THE FULL CIRCLE

1255

Young
Adult

THE

illustrated by the author

FULL CIRCLE

BY YOSHIKO UCHIDA

FRIENDSHIP PRESS

NEW YORK

First printing April 1957
Second printing August 1957

Copyright, 1957, by Friendship Press, Inc.
Library of Congress Catalog Card Number 57-6165

PRINTED IN THE UNITED STATES OF AMERICA

FOR LOUISE DeFOREST

PREFACE

To be the daughter of a famous man may be exciting, but it is not always easy. In this book I have told the story of Umeko, the youngest daughter of Dr. Toyohiko Kagawa, one of Japan's best known Christian leaders. It tells of the years during World War II when Umeko was in her teens, but it is not the story of a typical Japanese teen-ager. Umeko's family is a unique one, even among Christians in Japan.

Some of the problems she faced arose because of her father's prominence and devotion to his work. I believe, however, that many of her hopes and dilemmas are shared by teen-agers the world over and that her problems in adjusting to a postwar world are similar to those that confront many young people in Japan.

Although the book was suggested by experiences that Umeko shared with me, many of the events described and all the major characters, with the exception of her family, are fictional. Also, experiences that actually covered a broad span of years have had to be telescoped, and many of the wartime hardships endured by Dr. Kagawa, in particular, were actually much more trying than could be depicted in this book.

I am grateful to Dr. and Mrs. Kagawa for their willingness to let me write this book about their daughter, and I am especially indebted to Umeko herself for her help in providing material for this story.

YOSHIKO UCHIDA

Oakland, California
January, 1957

U MEKO TOOK A SEARING GULP OF HOT BEAN SOUP AND blinked as she felt its warmth race down to her toes. She wiggled them appreciatively and hurried through breakfast, looking up at the calendar as she ate. She remembered the day she had circled November 3 with a red crayon. That was back in April when she was still only eleven and had just begun her first year at Keisen Girls' School. The older girls had told her then about Founder's Day in November, and she had come straight home and marked it on the kitchen calendar. It was hard to believe that at last it was November 3 ——1941.

"Just think," Umeko murmured, her mouth half full of rice.

Her mother looked up, waiting for her to go on.

"No classes all day. Games in the morning, and then the

bazaar and play after lunch." Umeko sighed happily and went on listing the events of Founder's Day as though her mother hadn't already heard them a hundred times.

For weeks now the girls at Keisen had been making doilies and cushions and scarves for the bazaar and planning for the athletic meet and the classroom displays. Umeko had, in addition, a part in the school play, and for days she had marched about the house reciting her lines in sonorous tones, announcing dramatically that she was Lord Hasegawa of the thirteenth century Royal Court.

"Mother!" Umeko exclaimed suddenly. "Suppose I forget my lines! Suppose I forget what to say! I'll simply die!" The thought made her stomach quiver, but her mother quickly comforted her.

"Now stop worrying, Ume Chan," she said. "You know your lines perfectly well, and I'm sure you won't forget them."

She handed Umeko the piece of toast her daughter always liked to have after her rice and soup, but Umeko shook her head.

"I can't eat it," she said. Her appetite had vanished as suddenly as the spring mist.

"You'll be sure to come in time for lunch, won't you?" she reminded her mother. "They'll be selling all kinds of good things."

"I'll come just as soon as I can," Mrs. Kagawa promised. "But with your father coming home from America so soon, I seem to have mountains of work to do." Before she could say more, the sound of a caller's voice came from the entrance.

Umeko heard their maid, Hana, hurrying down the hall in her bare feet and calling, "*Hai, hai!*" as she ran. Soon she returned saying, "It is a gentleman who would like to know when *Sensei* will be back. Will you talk to him?"

"Yes. Thank you, Hana San," Mrs. Kagawa said, and she rose quickly.

Umeko sighed as she watched her go. Father hadn't even set foot in Japan, but already people were beginning to come. When he did get back, the house would probably bulge again with callers from morning till night.

"Don't forget to come early!" Umeko called after her mother.

"All right, Ume Chan. All right," her mother answered as she disappeared down the hall.

Umeko glanced at the clock and leaped up. "Hana San! Where's my jacket?" she called. "I'm late! Where did I leave my shoes? Hana San, help me!"

But Hana had been helping at the Kagawa home for many years now, and she knew better than to let Umeko get her flustered. She moved slowly, wiping her hands on her big white apron.

"Your jacket is right here on the hook," she said quietly. "And your shoes are at the side entrance, just where you left them. Now calm yourself, and don't run all the way," she cautioned.

"I won't. Don't let Mother be late! Good-by!" Umeko called, as she burst from the house and raced down the walk and into the street.

Umeko always hurried until she passed the fragile wooden houses clustered together as though each was holding up the one next to it. The streets seemed strangely quiet today, and Umeko noticed that not only the *geta* maker but also the bean curd man and the old man who made the straw floor mats had left up their wooden night shutters. Umeko saw the

3

red and white flags fluttering at several gates, and then she remembered. Why, of course, it was Emperor Meiji's birthday! All Japan had a holiday today!

When the houses dwindled and the countryside seemed to break away from the grasp of the city, Umeko slowed down and took a deep breath. She was glad she lived on the outskirts of Tokyo and not in the middle of the bustling city. She walked slowly, past the thicket of swaying green bamboo, past the grove of cedar and pine where, in February, she came each year to look for the first red camellias blooming in the snow. Now she could see the fields of rice beyond, tall and golden and ready for harvesting. Already she could see sedge hats bobbing out in the fields as farmers pumped their wooden threshing machines. Their wives were out in the fields beside them, many of them with babies tied to their swaying backs.

"Ohayo! Good morning!" Umeko called, and the women nodded and waved as she passed.

Umeko walked on, looking at the bright persimmons dangling like tiny orange balloons from dark bare branches. She looked up at the vast blueness of the sky, and far out to the foot of the mountains where red and yellow maples stood bright against the darkness of the pine trees.

"Autumn is so wonderful," she sighed, and for a moment she felt the makings of a *haiku* poem welling up inside, but this was soon swept aside by a hundred other thoughts.

Umeko passed the old house where her family had lived before they moved next to Father's church and kindergarten. She remembered how crowded this old house had become with the students and ministers and sick people her father brought home almost every day until they had finally decided to move, leaving their home to these needy people.

4

When Umeko turned at the bend in the road, she saw Kazu Takahashi waiting for her. She was glad that her best friend lived on the way to school so they could walk part way together every day.

Kazu waved and ran toward her. "My mother's coming!" she called. "Is yours?"

Umeko nodded. "She promised to come for lunch, and she's staying to see us in the play," Umeko answered enthusiastically. "Can your mother stay, too?"

The smile vanished from Kazu's lips. "Only for lunch," she replied. "And Father didn't even want her to do that. He says it's the busiest time of the year now, and she shouldn't waste time away from the fields."

Umeko understood. Kazu's father had never approved of her going to Keisen in the first place. "What will you learn at a Christian school?" he had asked. "It is far better that you remain a good Buddhist like your father." In the end he had given in, but only because Keisen was the nearest school.

The two girls walked on down the road. "I guess most of the other girls will have both parents there for the whole day," Umeko said, with a note of envy in her voice.

"But your father's been lecturing in America," Kazu said quickly. "He couldn't come even if he wanted to."

"I know," Umeko said glumly. "But he'd probably be too busy to come even if he were right here in Tokyo."

Kazu glanced at Umeko. "But he's an important man," she said. "I guess he can't help it if he's so busy."

Kazu waited for Umeko to say something more, but Umeko had turned away. She was looking out toward the hills, busy with her own secret thoughts, and the girls walked the rest of the way to school in silence.

The morning flickered away like a sigh. Umeko and Kazu

worked in the auditorium, helping with the sets and costumes for the play. Occasionally, a head would pop in to shout, "The third year girls just won the relay!" or "The second year girls won the hundred meter dash!"

And after a while someone called, "Kazu Takahashi! Your mother's outside."

Kazu glanced at the clock. "My goodness!" she exclaimed. "It's lunch time already."

"If your mother's here, mine must be, too," Umeko said hopefully, and together they hurried to the school grounds. They could see Mrs. Takahashi seated beneath the golden gingko tree, wiping her sun-tanned face with a big white handkerchief. She had changed from her gray field clothes to her good silk kimono and wore her best *geta*. She smiled as she saw Kazu and Umeko running toward her.

"Am I late?" she asked anxiously. "So many parents seem to be here already."

"Oh, no," Umeko reassured her. "My mother hasn't even come yet!"

Mrs. Takahashi sighed. "Ah, that is good," she said, and she sat back to enjoy the festive sight.

Beyond the school building she could see the row of wooden stalls that had been erected and draped with red and white bunting. In these stalls girls were selling steaming hot noodles, fancy vinegared rice balls, sweet bean-paste cakes, and toasted chestnuts. Umeko followed Mrs. Takahashi's glance and wished her mother would hurry.

"It's so nice to forget about everything for a while," Kazu's mother said softly. "About the work in the fields, and the war in China."

Umeko knew she was thinking of Kazu's brother who had been drafted and sent to fight in China six months ago.

6

"We don't talk much about the war here at Keisen, do we, Umeko?" Kazu asked.

Umeko shook her head. "Hardly at all! And no more drilling and marching and memorizing those long behavior codes!" she added with a grin, remembering their days at Asahi Elementary School.

"And no more scoldings for you!" Kazu went on.

"Thank goodness!" Umeko said, for at Asahi she'd been rebuked many times for not having a family shrine at home. "Remember the time I got caught looking up when I was supposed to be bowing at forty-five degrees?" she asked.

"The day the principal marched into assembly with the Emperor's photograph?" Kazu interrupted.

Umeko nodded. "I can still see him holding that picture stretched up above his head so his breath wouldn't defile it!"

Kazu and Umeko laughed as they remembered the militaristic air that had hovered over Asahi Elementary School, but Mrs. Takahashi remained solemn. She knew such militarism could grow in frightening directions.

Suddenly one of their classmates called to them, "You'd better hurry if you want something to eat! The food's almost sold out!"

Coming closer, the girl bowed to Mrs. Takahashi and then turned to Umeko. "I thought you said your mother was coming," she said.

"She is!" Umeko answered a bit annoyed. "She is coming!" she added insistently.

But when it was one o'clock and Mrs. Kagawa had not come, they decided they must eat without her.

"Don't worry, Umeko Chan," Mrs. Takahashi consoled her. "She'll surely come in time for the play."

Umeko nodded, but the rice ball with the sliver of tuna

seemed to have no taste at all, and the sweet bean-paste cake seemed to stick in her throat.

"Where's your mother, Umeko?" everyone asked, and each time Umeko wished she had never told her friends that her mother would come. She might have known something would happen so her mother could not keep her promise.

"Come inside with us," Mrs. Takahashi urged. "I just have time to visit the bazaar before I must leave."

But Umeko shook her head. "I think I'll wait outside just a little longer," she said.

When Kazu and her mother had gone inside, Umeko ran once more to look down the road. It looked hot and dusty in the sun, and there was no one on it but a farmer leading an old black ox.

Umeko bit her lip and went to the auditorium to get dressed for the play. She stood apart from the other whispering, giggling girls who kept running to the curtain to look for their parents.

Soon Kazu was beside Umeko. "Hasn't she come?" she asked.

"I don't think she's coming at all," Umeko answered darkly, and, somehow, even her beautiful costume of pale green gauze with its gold embroidery failed to conjure its usual magic. Umeko couldn't have felt less like a dignified court nobleman. She felt only like the disappointed twelve-year-old that she was.

When the play was over, Umeko took the curtain call with the cast, bowing and smiling and feeling a sudden surge of happiness. It was wonderful to be applauded and admired, and she promptly announced to Kazu that she thought she'd like to become an actress.

"Think what people would say!" she said, grinning impu-

8

dently. "And think of the commotion it would cause at home." It was a thought that made her giggle with delight.

Just as they hurried back to their classroom to get their jackets, they ran into Umeko's mother rushing down the hall.

"Mother!" Umeko cried. "What happened? I waited all morning for you!"

Mrs. Kagawa wiped her face and took a deep breath. "I'm so sorry, Ume Chan," she panted. "I ran almost all the way." She sank down on a bench and sighed wearily, "Such a terrible morning!"

"What happened?" Kazu asked. "Is something wrong?"

"Well, I was just ready to leave at eleven o'clock when someone called at the front entrance," Umeko's mother began. "Hana San was busy, so I went to the door, and there stood a man with a wild look in his eyes, holding a gun!"

Umeko and Kazu gasped together, "A gun! Was he a thief?"

"No, thank goodness," Mrs. Kagawa went on, "but he was so upset, he scarcely knew what he was doing. He asked me to pray with him before he killed himself."

"At our house?" Umeko exploded. "Why did he have to come to our house to do that? And today of all days!"

"He had met your father and had come to him once before for help," her mother explained quietly. "You see, he'd just had word that his son was killed in China. He lost his wife only last year. He was crazed with grief, Ume Chan, and I couldn't leave until he had quieted down and agreed to leave his gun with me."

Umeko could almost see this wild, fear-ridden man, and she shuddered at the thought. Well, Mother and Father might spend their lives taking care of people like that, but she wouldn't! She was going to enjoy life!

9

"I'm afraid I've missed your play," her mother apologized. "I know how much it meant to you, and I am so sorry."

"But the bazaar's still going on," Kazu added brightly. "You haven't missed everything."

But so far as Umeko was concerned, the whole day had been spoiled and when they left, she walked home with Mother in glum silence. Mother asked about the lunch and the play and the games, but Umeko knew her mind was really on all the things that had to be done at home. She knew Mother wanted to do the big annual house cleaning before Father returned, even if Tokyo's official cleaning day did come later. Umeko knew all the floor mats would be taken out and beaten, that the woodwork would be scrubbed, the quilts aired and sunned, and the whole house cleaned from top to bottom.

Soon they could see the steeple of their church rising above the gray tiled roofs, and as they approached the gate to their house, they could hear the sound of quilts being beaten out in the yard.

"Ah, that must be Toshio San helping Hana San," Mother said gratefully.

Toshio was the college student who had lived with them for so long, he had become another big brother to Umeko, especially since her own brother, as well as her sister, had gone away to medical school.

"Ah-ha! Here comes the great actress," Toshio called out to tease Umeko. "Did you remember your lines and act properly dignified?"

"'Course, I did," Umeko answered, "but Mother didn't see me. She missed everything." Umeko stood drawing circles in the dirt with her toe.

Toshio stopped beating the quilts. "Why? What happened?" he asked.

"It was an unfortunate emergency," Mrs. Kagawa explained as she hurried into the house. But Umeko told Toshio all about the man with the gun.

"Ah, that was too bad," Toshio said sympathetically. "But I suppose your mother had no choice."

"People like that are always coming and spoiling everything!" Umeko muttered. "Sometimes I just wish no one had ever heard of Father. I wish he were a carpenter or a noodle vendor or something." Umeko felt herself growing hot and flustered.

Toshio looked amused and then began to laugh. "Don't be a difficult adolescent, Umeko!" he said. "You know very well you're proud of your father. Look at the work he's done in the slums and the cooperatives and the settlements and labor unions, and . . . . "

"I know, I know," Umeko interrupted. "Don't preach to me!"

But Toshio paid no attention to her. "And look at me," he went on. "Where would I be if your father hadn't helped me? I'd probably be one of those filthy, red-eyed beggars, sleeping at Ueno Station, picking up rags and cigarette butts in order to eat."

Toshio twisted his face into a horrible grimace and hobbled about picking up imaginary cigarette butts, holding out a shaky hand to Umeko for money.

Umeko laughed in spite of herself. "Stop it!" she shouted. "You look horrible!"

She remembered the cold, rainy night Father had brought Toshio home. He had been a thin, hungry child who had run away from his uncle in Hokkaido. Umeko recalled how he sobbed out his story, telling them how all his family had died of tuberculosis and he had been left to live with an uncle who had too many children of his own. He had been so miserable, he had finally run away, managing somehow to get as far as Tokyo. Father found him roaming around the station, hungry and cold and frightened. He had brought him home, and Toshio had lived with them ever since.

"You know what your big trouble is?" Toshio asked her suddenly.

"What?" asked Umeko.

"You're just feeling sorry for yourself, that's all," he said firmly. "Now hurry inside and help your mother. You know she has lots to do before your father gets home. And you're not helping me get the quilts beaten!"

"Don't tell me what to do," Umeko began with an insolent grin, but when she saw Toshio raise his bamboo rod in the air and move menacingly toward her, she ran into the house laughing and screaming, "Help! Toshio San's trying to beat me!"

Already, Mother was in Father's study answering some letters, and Hana was busy upstairs. Umeko went to the kitchen to look for something to eat and noticed another red circle on the calendar. She bent forward for a closer look. The circle was around November 7, and beside it Mother had scribbled, "Father home." Just four more days and Father would be back from America! Umeko looked down at the new red sweater she wore, wondering vaguely what Father would say when he saw it.

CHAPTER TWO

FROM THE MOMENT SHE WENT DOWNSTAIRS FOR BREAKFAST, Umeko could feel the difference. The house had a changed air. It was like a clock wound up taut and tight, ready to begin ticking busily the moment Father got home. Mother had eaten early, and Hana had already begun her usual morning cleaning. Umeko could hear the sound of her duster beating the books in Father's study, and she knew that soon Hana would scatter wet tea leaves over the *tatami* and sweep vigorously with her big, floppy broom.

Since Umeko went to school, she couldn't go with Mother to Yokohama to meet the ship, but she knew that by the time she got home Father would probably be there. She felt excited and yet a little anxious. Father was always so busy with his work, sometimes Umeko felt that she really did not know him very well—at least, not well enough to confide in

13

him the hopes and problems that were all tangled up inside of her. They seemed so unimportant compared with his work.

The telephone rang sharply, jolting Umeko from her thoughts. Then someone was at the front door calling, "*Gomen kudasai* . . . Excuse me!" It sounded like one of the men who helped Father with his work. Umeko could hear Mother and Hana hurrying down the hall, and then there were more voices at the entrance. It was going to be a busy day. Umeko finished her breakfast quickly and hurried off to school.

When she got home that afternoon, she knew Father was there. Placed neatly in the front entrance she saw those scuffed black shoes she'd know anywhere. Umeko looked carefully at the other shoes and *geta*, for she could usually tell who was inside by the footwear at the entrance.

"Let's see," she murmured, examining them carefully, but today it was too hard to match shoes and faces, and she hurried inside, skirting boxes and cartons that she knew were filled with books belonging to her father.

Umeko heard the dull hum of voices in the study. She took a deep breath, knocked, and looked in. The room seemed to overflow with people.

"Father," she called. "Welcome home!"

Dr. Kagawa was surrounded by people, but he rose and came to greet her. "It's good to see you, Ume Chan," he said with a warm smile. "You've grown since I last saw you. Are you enjoying school?"

Umeko nodded. "Yes," she answered, "but I still don't like the homework!"

"Ume Chan, why don't you make us all some tea?" Mother suggested. She knew Umeko enjoyed preparing ceremonial tea, and this was a good way to give her something to do while Dr. Kagawa continued his conversation with his visitors.

"In here?" Umeko asked. Father's study was furnished with a dark round table and blue upholstered chairs. Somehow it didn't seem proper to make tea in here. She thought of her tea ceremony teacher's home, where they sat on the neat, cream-colored *tatami*, their legs tucked carefully under them. Beside them was the small sunken hearth where water simmered gently in an iron kettle. Umeko grinned as she thought how shocked her teacher would be to see her serving tea sitting in a chair, her legs dangling, and the hot water in the kettle on top of the table.

"This doesn't feel right," Umeko said with a giggle.

But Mother urged her to go on. "Never mind," she said, "the tea will taste just as good, and you can prepare and serve it properly some other time."

Umeko prepared one cup of tea at a time. She whipped the powdered tea to a pale green froth with her tiny bamboo brush, gathered the bubbles at the center, and turned the cup as she presented it to the first guest. There was a proper motion for every step, and Umeko concentrated hard, listening only vaguely to the conversation that flowed around her.

Everyone seemed eager to hear about America. "What did the Americans say, *Sensei?* Were they talking of going to war? What did they say about our militarists?"

Umeko looked up at the mention of war. The papers were full of anti-American sentiment, and ugly rumors of war seemed to be sifting into their lives with alarming speed.

"But how can we possibly fight America?" Umeko asked herself. "We're already busy fighting one war in China."

Umeko was to hear much more of this kind of talk, however, for it arose whenever someone came to see her father, and that was discouragingly often. There were rarely less than ten guests at supper every night.

One of Umeko's chores was to help Hana set the table for supper, and each afternoon she would go reluctantly to the kitchen to ask, "How many tonight, Hana San?"

Sometimes Hana would say, "Only nine tonight." More often, however, she would say, "Set fifteen places, please," or "Seventeen tonight, Umeko Chan," or even "Twenty!"

Umeko would groan as she arranged the chopsticks at each place, saying fiercely, "We'll be doing dishes all night, and I hate drying dishes!"

But Hana would simply laugh at her and say, "It's good practice for you. Some day you'll have a home of your own, then you'll be glad you've had this experience."

Umeko would make a face and answer haughtily, "Oh, I may not get married at all. I may decide to live alone and write a great novel . . . or maybe I'll become an actress."

Then Hana would laugh even harder. "Ah, Umeko Chan, you won't be talking like that a few years from now. You wait and see."

One day, when Umeko asked how many places to set for dinner, Hana smiled. "You'll be pleased," she said, "only the family and the Suzukis tonight."

Why, that's just like family only, Umeko thought, and she actually enjoyed putting the soy sauce and pickled radishes out on the table. Mr. Suzuki was superintendent of their church kindergarten, and Mrs. Suzuki was one of their best teachers. The Suzukis had been with the kindergarten ever since her father first organized it, and to Umeko they had been like a real aunt and uncle. She thought Mr. Suzuki with his round, friendly face and Mrs. Suzuki with her gentle ways were two of the finest people she knew. It'll be a good supper tonight, she thought confidently.

When they were all seated at the table, however, Umeko

noticed that Mr. Suzuki looked at Father with a worried frown on his face.

"How did it go today, *Sensei?*" he asked. "We thought of you all day."

Umeko noticed that Father looked solemn and rather sad. "Well, I did my best," he answered slowly, "but the voice of the pacifist is not popular today. Those who talk of peace are labeled traitors."

Mr. Suzuki nodded. "If we could only get our country out of the militarists' control," he said despondently.

Umeko wondered what they were talking about. Where had Father gone to do his best? What had he done today? She leaned toward Toshio and whispered, "Do you know what they're talking about?"

But Toshio only shrugged and shook his head. He leaned forward to hear more of their conversation.

Umeko turned to her mother. She was too curious to care about being impolite. "Where did Father go?" she asked in a loud whisper. "What in the world are they talking about?"

Mother explained in an undertone that her father had appeared before the House of Representatives and the House of Peers to urge that all thoughts of war with America be abandoned.

So that was it. "But we're not really going to fight the United States, are we?" Umeko asked.

"I hope not," her mother answered quietly. "With all my heart, I hope not."

But as Umeko glanced at the faces around the table, she knew that everyone feared the worst. It wasn't turning out to be a very pleasant supper after all.

The next Sunday the strength of the militarists was to make itself felt right in the Kagawa home. Umeko was up early, for there was always much to do on Sunday mornings. First, it was necessary to clear the rooms in their house so the Sunday school classes could use them. Then, it was her task to place at the chapel entrance slippers for the people to put on when they removed their shoes.

Umeko had put on her navy blue wool, remembering the times she'd been reprimanded by her father for wearing a bright-colored dress on Sundays.

"Live and dress simply, Ume Chan," he always said to her. "It is only by living simply that we can see the beauty of God."

"But, Father," Umeko would object, "all the girls wear bright dresses—and jewelry, too!"

Then Father would usually answer, "It's what is inside of you that matters, Ume Chan. Never mind the outside. Don't garnish yourself with trinkets like a cannibal."

Umeko disliked being lectured. "What's wrong with cannibals?" she retorted one day. "They're human beings, too."

But her mother had quickly put a stop to the argument. "Don't argue with your father," she had said. "He wants us to live simple, humble lives, and we must respect his wishes."

"Well, maybe, when I'm fifty-three I won't mind," Umeko had said gloomily, "but it's no fun when I'm twelve."

Mother smiled. "I know it's difficult," she said, "but you try. And remember," she added, "your father may not always show his love and affection for you openly, but it's only because he doesn't know how, and not because he doesn't care for you."

Then she would tell Umeko about the unhappiness that had filled her father's childhood and the struggles of his youth, and Umeko would try to understand why her father seemed so stern at times.

At any rate, Umeko couldn't help disliking the somber

colors she was asked to wear, and now she examined herself distastefully, turning this way and that in front of her mirror. There she was, plain and dull—straight hair pulled down into two braids, a loose-fitting dark dress with a round white collar, and cotton lisle stockings for warmth. Not a trace of color, much less glamour, anywhere! Umeko suddenly opened her dresser drawer, took out the red camellia pin, and fastened it securely at her collar.

"There! I look much better," she murmured, and she felt a delicious excitement in her wickedness. She felt the same way whenever she stayed up late to read novels she'd been forbidden to read. But this was something in which Kazu indulged with equal guilt.

"Only I don't sneak up salted rice cakes to eat while I read," Kazu would say. It was wonderful, the things that Umeko could do now that her sister was away at medical school and she had the room all to herself. Eating rice cakes while she read was nice, but being able to keep the hot water bottle to herself all night was equally delightful.

Umeko touched the pin at her throat and then hurried out of the house before her father could see her. She went to the chapel and arranged the slippers in neat rows so people could remove their shoes and *geta* and slip into them quickly.

"There! That's done," she said to herself as she hurried to her own Sunday school class.

Classes usually ended before the church service, and Umeko would sit outside with her friends, waiting to hear the sound of the closing hymn. Soon after, there would be a silence for the benediction, and then, as the small reed organ played, the adults would file out into the sunshine, bowing to one another and blinking in the brightness.

But today a long silence followed the closing hymn. The

organ remained silent, and none of the congregation came out.

"That's queer," Umeko muttered. "I wonder what's going on?"

Just then she saw her father emerge from the chapel with two strange men, one on either side of him. They held him by the arms, as though they were afraid he might try to slip away. Their faces were grim, and they remained silent as they led Dr. Kagawa toward the street.

"Father!" Umeko cried. "Where are they taking you?"

Umeko's father turned and smiled faintly. "Don't worry, Ume Chan," he said quietly. "Everything will be all right. I'll be back."

Umeko ran to the front gate and watched as the men led her father into a black car and then drove speedily away.

Now everyone streamed from the chapel, looking frightened, and the buzz of anxious conversation seemed to surround Umeko. She tried to get to her mother, but it was no use. Then she saw Toshio.

"Toshio San!" she called, and, tugging at his sleeve, she drew him to the edge of the crowd. Soon he was surrounded by the girls in Umeko's class.

"What happened, Toshio San?" they all asked at once. "Who were those men? Where are they taking Sensei?"

"Well," Toshio began slowly, "right after the benediction, two strange men marched down the aisle from the rear. They went up to Sensei just as he was putting away some of the charts he had used in the sermon and told him he must come immediately for questioning. They were military police in civilian clothing."

A small gasp circled the listening girls. "The military police!" they cried in high frightened voices.

"They didn't even let Sensei finish what he was doing or

stop to talk to Mrs. Kagawa or the Suzukis," Toshio continued indignantly. "They just took him by both arms and marched him down the aisle of the church."

"In front of everybody?" Umeko asked.

Toshio nodded. "They told us to stay seated, and we were all too stunned to move or say a word. I suppose we were sitting there with our mouths hanging open!"

"I wonder if they sat through all of Father's sermon?" Umeko said.

"I'm sure of it," Toshio answered. "I think they sat in the last row and heard every word."

"And did *Sensei* talk about America?" the girls wondered.

"I'm afraid he did," Toshio said slowly. "He told about Christians in America who are praying with us that war between our two countries may never come. He urged us to continue to pray for peace," Toshio added. "It was his usual plea."

"No wonder the military police dragged him off," Umeko murmured. "But I suppose Father knew they'd be coming some day."

"Well, don't you worry," Toshio said reassuringly. "He won't let them frighten him. He's been questioned before. He'll be back soon. You wait and see."

At lunch time, everyone said the same thing, "He'll be back soon." "We'll get help from people who can obtain his release," Mr. Suzuki added.

The Suzukis and several of the church deacons stayed for lunch, talking together in hushed voices as though the secret police might be hiding in the walls. Mother appeared calm, but Umeko noticed that she wasn't eating her lunch. In fact, no one seemed to have much of an appetite.

Umeko saw her mother put down her chopsticks. "The thing I fear most is that the questioning will not stop with just

21

our family," she said slowly. "The military government seems to believe that all Christians are pro-West and, consequently, traitors to Japan."

"If we could only make them see that for us God comes first, before our country or our Emperor," Mrs. Suzuki sighed. "But I fear they will never understand."

Now Mr. Suzuki had stopped eating. He cleared his throat and spoke slowly. "I didn't want to speak of this—especially today—but since the problem has come up. . . ."

Umeko wondered what in the world he was about to say. She had never seen him look so troubled.

"I have already been questioned by the police," he said. "And although they didn't detain me, they suggested it would be wise for me to stop teaching here and to leave the city." Mr. Suzuki rubbed his forehead. "Apparently, my teaching is considered a bad influence on the children."

Umeko's mother gasped. "So it has come to this already!" she said sadly. "I had hoped the rest of you would be spared."

"But what will you do?" the others asked Mr. Suzuki. "Where will you go?"

"We thought we would go to Akagi Village, my old home," Mrs. Suzuki explained. "It is a small farming community in the mountains, and we could do much to help the villagers."

They all listened and shook their heads gravely. "If Suzuki San has been told to leave, then surely Kagawa *Sensei* must leave Tokyo, too. Surely the police. . . ."

And then they stopped, remembering that Umeko was there. Giving her quick reassuring smiles, they said, "It will all work out somehow."

Mrs. Kagawa made arrangements for the assistant pastor to conduct the evening service and went for her shawl. She and Mr. Suzuki were going to see about getting Father released.

"We'll have to make several calls," she explained to Umeko. "Help Hana San with the dishes, won't you?"

Umeko nodded absently. Everyone bowed to say farewell, and then, still talking in serious whispers, they drifted away. Toshio, too, took his books and went off to the library. The house that had bustled with activity suddenly seemed to sag with quiet and emptiness like a spent balloon.

Umeko carried the dishes out to the kitchen where Hana had begun to wash the pans under the cold running water.

"I've put a pan of water on the burner," she said cheerfully. "The dishes will be easier to dry if we rinse them in hot water."

Umeko knew Hana was being especially good to her, but she could think of nothing nice to say to her in return. Instead, she simply said, "They're still a lot of bother, and I hate drying dishes!"

After that they finished the dishes in silence.

When Umeko went upstairs to her room, she found the afternoon sun streaming in the window, making square patches of light on her *tatami*. She had left her homework till the last minute, but as she sat at her desk and opened her algebra book, the thought of doing her problems was too odious to contemplate. Umeko glanced at her closet. No one's home, she thought. Why not? It won't hurt for just a while.

Umeko opened her closet door, thrust her hand between the folded quilts, and pulled out *The Tales of Genji*. She lay on her stomach, dipped her hand into a bag of salted rice crackers, and began to read. It was wonderful not to have to be watchful about making too much noise as she turned the pages or chewed her crackers.

Umeko read until her room grew dark with shadows. She looked at the clock. Five o'clock! She hurried downstairs, but there was no sign at all of her mother.

"Hana San," she called, but the house was silent. She went to the back door and saw that Hana's *geta* were gone. She'd probably gone out to buy something for supper. The house suddenly seemed full of shadows and creaks, and her own footsteps echoed strangely in the stillness. Umeko shivered. She didn't like being in a silent house alone at dusk. Suppose another despondent man with a gun should appear!

"I wish somebody would come home," she murmured to herself. She wished her brother and sister hadn't both gone off to medical school. She wished Toshio had stayed home. She wished her mother would hurry back.

Umeko wandered back upstairs and sat on the plum-colored cushion before her small, low dresser, peering at her face in the half-darkness. She pulled her hair up at the side, wondering how she would look with short curly hair. If Father would only let me have a permanent, she thought wistfully. She pulled her hair up and back to see how she might look when she was forty-five. Horrible! Umeko made a face at herself, and then her eye fell on the red pin. So much had happened, she'd forgotten until now that she was wearing it. She wondered if Mother and the others had noticed it at lunch, and suddenly she felt full of remorse and guilt. She had been wicked to disobey her father deliberately, and on Sunday of all days!

Umeko hurriedly unfastened the pin and put it back in its cotton-padded box. She was glad Father hadn't seen it before he was taken away. Now that the pin was off, Umeko felt better. She felt sure everything would turn out all right. Maybe things would work out so the Suzukis could stay in Tokyo, too. As she heard the front gate slide open, she hurried downstairs.

"Mother!" she called. "When are they going to let Father come home?"

CHAPTER THREE

I THINK FATHER WILL BE RELEASED IN A WEEK OR TWO," Mother had assured Umeko that Sunday.

And it was just as she said. One day Umeko came home from school and found Father dictating letters in his study as though he'd been doing that every day for the past two weeks. He looked tired, but he said nothing about what had happened to him. Even when he came to supper, he acted as though he had not been away at all. This wasn't especially strange to Umeko, however, for her father seldom spoke of himself or about what he had done. Instead, he spoke of the needs of the people at his settlement houses, or of cooperatives, or of the Friends of Jesus who were seeking to win a million Christians in Japan.

"The more one is blessed, the more one owes the world," he always said and plunged deeper than ever into his work.

One afternoon a few weeks after her father had returned, Umeko saw a big wagon standing beside their front gate. She hurried inside and saw that the glass doors along the veranda had all been pushed open. Instead of the beginning of winter, it looked like midsummer with the house opened wide to the cool green of the garden. Just inside the doors were tall, wavering stacks of Father's books, and behind them were four chairs, two bookcases, and an old roll-top desk.

That's strange, thought Umeko, Father's study was cleaned before he got back from America.

She went inside calling, "*Tadaima!* I'm home!" But no one seemed to hear her. She heard voices in the study, and then Hana staggered out with still another stack of books. She set them down beside the others and flicked the dust from them with her duster.

"My goodness," Umeko said as she watched, "are you cleaning house again?"

Hana remained silent a moment and then answered, "Well, yes. I guess you could call it that."

That was a strange answer. Umeko wondered about it as she went to the kitchen to look for something to eat. She found a bamboo basket filled with tangerines and took one, peeling it carefully to keep the hull in one piece. Then she hurried back to see what was going on.

Now Mother and Father emerged from the study, followed by two men in blue *happi* coats with towels tied around their heads. Umeko supposed they'd been called to do some carpentry work, but suddenly she saw a peculiar transaction. Instead of Father giving them money, one of the men carefully counted out several bills and handed them to Father. He nodded his thanks and then went upstairs as though he didn't want to have anything more to do with them. The two men walked straight to the furniture, picked up the desk, and marched out with it.

Umeko watched this strange performance and then called to her mother. "What's going on?" she asked. "What in the world is happening?"

"Why, Ume Chan, I didn't hear you come in," her mother said, looking startled. "Nothing special is going on. We're just disposing of some things your father no longer needs."

"Oh," Umeko said, but she thought of the money the man had given father. She pointed to the furniture. "Are we selling these things?" she asked. "Are we that poor now?"

Mrs. Kagawa smiled briefly. "We're not in dire need ourselves," she explained. "But the settlement houses need money, and Father thought this would be an excellent way to help them and clean house at the same time."

"But he has never sold things before to keep the settlement houses going," Umeko went on. "Why does he have to do that now?"

"Well, Ume Chan," Mother began slowly, "until now the books your father has written have brought in enough money for most of his work. But now the military government has banned the sale of all his books, and that has cut off a big portion of our income."

"Then nobody can buy any of Father's books in the bookstalls now?" Umeko asked. That meant about a hundred different books as far as Umeko knew.

Her mother nodded. "No one can buy them, and no one can sell them. They're considered pro-West, anti-Japanese, and a dangerous influence on the Japanese people," she explained.

"But how silly!" Umeko muttered. "What could be dangerous about Father's books!"

Her mother looked up as the two men returned for their last load. "It does seem foolish," she agreed, "but when those in power become afraid, then we can expect them to do many foolish and rash things."

In the days to come, Umeko was to learn how true this was.

IT WAS NOW THE TWELFTH MONTH OF 1941, AND TOKYO WAS cold, drab, and full of ominous rumblings of war. On the eighth day, just as Umeko had finished breakfast and was listening with the family to the morning newscast, an urgent voice broke in on the commentator.

"The day of liberation has come at last," he said proudly. "Our aircraft have just completed a surprise attack on the United States fleet at Pearl Harbor. Arise, fellow men of Asia! Japan will lead the way toward a Greater East Asia Co-Prosperity Sphere. . . ."

The voice went on, but everyone was too stunned to listen further. Umeko saw her father turn pale and bow his head. The war he had worked so hard to prevent had come. The two countries he loved must now fight each other, and one of them would have to lose.

"So it's come at last," Toshio whispered. His voice was tense and hard.

"Such a terrible mistake," Umeko's mother murmured. "A terrible mistake!"

Umeko's legs trembled as she walked to school, and she felt a strange confusion inside. Of course, she loved her own country, but she couldn't suddenly hate America as an enemy country. So many of the missionaries who had come to work in Japan were Americans. How could she possibly hate them?

At school there was a strange feeling in the air as the girls gathered in excited clusters in the hallway. It was as though each of them had brought along the feelings expressed at home. Some appeared frightened and spoke in tense anxious whispers, but many looked jubilant and spoke with enthusiasm and confidence.

Even Kazu was excited. "Father says the Americans are weak," she told Umeko. "He says we'll win the war in a few months and then Japan will be the leader of all Asia. He says we'll have a wonderful future."

"I don't know, Kazu . . . ," Umeko began. She tried to put into words the confusion she felt, but Kazu wasn't even listening. Someone else was telling how her brother had gone right out to volunteer for the army as soon as he had heard the news.

Umeko heard Kazu say proudly, "But my big brother is already in the army. He's fighting in China." And as she spoke, she held her head high.

A few days later Umeko discovered her father had cleaned out his study and packed his things.

"Have the military police told you to leave?" she asked.

Father nodded. "They've made it impossible for me to continue working in Tokyo," he explained. "I've decided it would be best for me to go to Teshima."

Umeko remembered well the lovely island in the Inland Sea where they had gone many times to visit the orphanage and school and sanatorium that her father had helped establish.

"I shall work at the sanatorium there," her father continued. "When there is time, I hope to do some writing. And, of course, I shall be among good friends."

And so, in a few days, Dr. Kagawa left for Osaka where he would catch the boat for Teshima.

Umeko and Toshio went to the station with Mrs. Kagawa to see him off. It was always exciting to go to Tokyo Station, but this was the first time Umeko had been there since the war broke out, and it seemed more crowded than ever before. Everywhere there were soldiers in khaki, shouldering big knapsacks and looking grim and solemn. Everywhere there were little knots of people, bowing, waving flags, and saying good-by.

As they edged toward the platform for the Osaka train, they passed groups of people singing military marches and shouting "Banzai." It was "Banzai" for the Emperor, "Banzai" for the homeland, and "Banzai" for the men going off to fight.

"It's almost like a big festival, isn't it?" Umeko called out to Toshio, but Toshio didn't reply. He watched tight-lipped as the soldiers bowed stiffly to those they left behind and boarded the train with their heads held high.

"*Sayonara!* Good-by! *Banzai! Banzai!*" the crowds shouted.

The platform was soon filled with pushing, shouting, singing people, and Umeko was barely able to see her father as he pushed his way onto the train.

"I'm afraid he will never find a seat," her mother murmured anxiously.

They tried to catch a glimpse of him as he moved up the aisle, but the windows were crowded with soldiers who leaned out for a last good-by.

"If he can't find a seat, he can always sit on his suitcase," Umeko suggested.

Her mother nodded. "I'm afraid that's exactly what he will have to do. It won't be comfortable for eight hours," she added with a sigh, "but I suppose it can't be helped."

"*Sayonara!* Take care of yourself!" Umeko shouted as she waved. She wasn't sure that Father had seen her at all, but dozens of other hands waved back to her. And now the train slowly got under way. The voices of the crowd grew more

30

urgent. "Take care of yourself! Be careful! *Sayonara!*" they shouted, waving handkerchiefs and flags until the last car had pulled out, and the train sped down the tracks in a cloud of steam and smoke.

And then a sudden quiet came over the platform. The people who had been shouting and waving were silent, and the women who had been waving flags rolled them up and held handkerchiefs to their eyes. Umeko knew now that it was not like a festival at all. Some of these very soldiers she had seen today might never come back at all. She looked at Toshio, but he didn't even seem to know she was there. He stood gazing down the tracks after the train, his fists clenched hard.

"Toshio San!" Umeko called, but he didn't even turn.

Only when Umeko's mother put a hand on his shoulder did he turn suddenly as though someone had just awakened him.

"Shall we start for home?" she asked gently.

Toshio nodded. "Yes, yes, of course," he murmured and strode quickly toward the exit.

By the time they reached home, it had already grown dark, and they could feel the sting of winter in the north wind. Hana waited for them with hot charcoal in the brazier and bean-curd soup bubbling on the stove.

"Brrrrr. I'm freezing!" Umeko shivered, and she ran to the brazier, warming her palms on its smooth round rim.

"Some of those soldiers will never feel the warmth of a brazier again," Toshio said grimly, and the look in his eyes suddenly made Umeko draw her own hands away.

Somehow, from that day, a change seemed to come over Toshio. Umeko would find him looking vacantly into the distance when he was supposed to be reading or even when he was having supper with them. Sometimes she would have to call him twice before he realized she had said something.

31

"What do you suppose is wrong with Toshio San?" Umeko asked her mother.

"A young man in a country at war has a great many problems he must face, Ume Chan," her mother explained. "Just leave him alone, and he'll tell us about them when he's ready."

Christmas came quietly, and the church had its program without Dr. Kagawa or Mr. Suzuki. They lit candles and sang the old familiar carols and prayed that peace might come once more to earth. And still Toshio had little to say to Umeko or her mother. Instead, he seemed to spend more and more time away from home with his school friends.

But soon it was time for winter recess at school, and Umeko wondered less about Toshio, for now all the excitement of the end of the year began to press close about her.

A week before New Year's Day, Hana and Mother began to scrub the woodwork and the *tatami* and to paste new rice paper on the *shoji* doors. The kitchen seemed to bulge with heavy white slabs of rice paste that friends brought as New Year's gifts, and Hana cut them up in small squares and stored them away carefully for New Year's broth. She knew, too, that if they were toasted and dipped in soy sauce and sugar, Toshio and Umeko could eat up the whole lot just between the two of them.

"Mmmmm," Umeko murmured as she inspected the kitchen. "Makes my mouth water just thinking about New Year's."

And as New Year's grew closer, Umeko's trips to the kitchen became more and more frequent. All day long Hana's knife would chatter busily on the cutting board, and, at the day's end, she would produce all sorts of delicacies to add to the tiered lacquer boxes in which food for the first three days of the new year was stored. Umeko couldn't resist lifting the lid and sniffing the delectable scent of soy sauce and sugar in which black beans, bamboo shoots, lotus root, fish paste, burdock root, knots of shiny seaweed, and a myriad other things had been cooked.

On the thirty-first of December, Hana announced that she was going to the fish shop to get a sea bream. "Want to come along?" she asked Umeko.

"'Course, I do!" Umeko answered, already reaching for her scarf. Seeing the hustle that surrounded the food shops on the last day of the year was something Umeko wouldn't miss for anything.

"Don't forget the pine and bamboo for our front gate," Mother reminded them as they left. "And will you get some plum blossoms for the front entrance, too?"

"All right," Umeko called. "If there're any left!"

But though the streets were thick with people all shopping for the same things, Umeko needn't have worried, for the streets were also filled with vendors who had set up little makeshift stalls to sell their New Year's wares. Bundled in sweaters and scarves and squatting beside small fires they had built to keep warm, they sold everything from branches of sweet-scented green pine to knots of twisted rope to be hung over one's gate to ward off the evil spirits.

As they passed the public bath house, Umeko could see people streaming in to emerge pink and clean for the new year. And as they walked along the streets, they could hear the sound of housewives sweeping their *tatami* and beating cushions and doing a final wash so that all the dust and dirt of the old year might be removed.

Even though Father and the Suzukis were away and her brother and sister were not able to get home from school, still it was New Year's, and Umeko felt gay and excited. Early on New Year's morning, she sprang from her quilts full of eager anticipation. It was fun to wear a kimono for a change, and Umeko struggled with the wide brocade sash as she tried to tie it herself.

"*Omedeto gozai masu* . . . Happy New Year!" she called as she went downstairs.

Toshio had stayed up late the night before to have his bowl of "passing-of-the-year-noodles" with his college friends, so he was still asleep. Only Mother and Hana were waiting for her.

They decided to let Toshio sleep, and it wasn't until long after they had had their New Year's breakfast and sampled all the delicacies in Hana's tiered boxes that Tosio came down.

"*Omedeto gozai masu* . . . Happy New Year!" he said solemnly, getting down on his knees as he bowed formally to Umeko's mother. "My thanks to you for all your kindnesses this past year."

He was grinning broadly and looked happier today than Umeko had seen him in a long time. In fact, he seemed to be his old cheerful self, and after having his New Year's breakfast, he even offered to play a game of battledore and shuttlecock with Umeko.

"You mean to say you'll actually play that little girls' game with me?" Umeko asked incredulously. She remembered how as a child she'd had to beg someone to play with her, for her brother and Toshio always wanted to go and fly their new kites and her sister went off to see her own friends.

"Sure, let's play a game just for old time's sake," Toshio said playfully. "And let's keep score."

"Oh, no, you don't," Umeko answered firmly, for she knew Toshio remembered how they used to keep score with charcoal, the winner marking his points on the loser's face.

"But, Umeko Chan, you might win. Revenge is sweet!" Toshio teased, but Umeko knew better than to give in. Toshio would hit the bright feathered shuttlecock many more times than she, and she wasn't taking any chances.

"No, thanks," she repeated. "Let's play!"

Just before they began, however, they heard Kazu calling from the gate. "Happy New Year," she shouted, and without even waiting for Umeko or Toshio to answer, she held up a cotton sash for them to see.

"Look what I've begun for my brother," she said. It was a good luck sash on which she would collect a thousand stitches from a thousand different people. Everyone was making them now to send to their soldiers for luck. "If my brother wears this," Kazu went on, "he'll be safe from harm. Here," she said, thrusting the sash toward Umeko, "will you add a stitch?"

"Of course, I will," Umeko said quickly. "Show me what to do."

But before Kazu could say more, Toshio reached for the sash. "Let me see it," he said, and, as he fingered it, his face grew solemn. "Will you girls make one for me when I go to war?" he asked with a faint smile.

"Why, of course, we will, Toshio San," Kazu promised.

"But you may not even have to go at all," Umeko added cheerfully. "Why, the war may be all over by the time you finish college."

"That's just what I'm afraid of," Toshio said, and suddenly his gaiety was gone. He handed to Kazu his fancy battledore trimmed with flowers of pink silk. "Here, you play with Umeko Chan," he said, and, turning toward the house, he called back, "See you later."

That night after supper, when all the guests who had come to make their New Year's calls had gone home, Toshio came to Umeko's mother.

"I've something to tell you," he began hesitantly.

Umeko and her mother both looked up. "Why, what is it, Toshio San?" Mrs. Kagawa asked, as she took off her reading glasses.

Toshio spoke in a low voice. "I want to tell you that I'm leaving school," he said. "I've volunteered for the army."

"Volunteered!" Umeko shouted. "But you can't do that! You've got to finish college."

Toshio shook his head. "I can't go on at school as though nothing had happened when other young men are going off to fight and die for our country," he said grimly.

"You're quite sure this is what you want to do?" Mother asked softly.

Toshio nodded. "Quite sure," he answered. "I've been thinking about it ever since the day we went to the station to see Sensei off for Osaka. When I saw those soldiers that day, I knew I couldn't sit back and go on studying as though nothing had happened. I knew I had to go, too. Two of my friends have volunteered with me. We went yesterday. Everything is settled, and I finally feel at peace with myself."

"Then I'm glad, Toshio San," Mrs. Kagawa said, putting a hand on his arm. "I know it wasn't an easy decision for you to make, but if you think it's right, that's all that matters."

"Thank you," Toshio said. "I'm glad you understand." And he rose quickly and went to his room.

In another week Toshio was ready to go. Umeko and her mother went once more to Tokyo Station, but this time it was Toshio to whom they waved good-by. He seemed cheerful and resolute. "Write me when you're not busy getting into trouble," he called to Umeko.

"I will," Umeko promised. "I'll even send you caramels! Good-by! Good luck!"

The people who crowded the platform shouted their fare-

36

wells all around Umeko and her mother. Then, as the train slowly pulled away, the flags were put aside, and the silent crowd moved slowly toward the stairs. Now, Toshio, too, was gone.

When Umeko got home from the station, she found a letter waiting for her on the hall table. The writing looked familiar, and she knew immediately it was that of her piano teacher, Miss Tanaka.

"Umeko San," she had written. "I do want to see you at the usual time next week, but don't bother to bring your music. I'll explain when I see you. Hastily, your friend, Kinuyo Tanaka."

That's queer, Umeko thought. She and Miss Tanaka did exchange letters occasionally, but only when they had something interesting to tell each other. This was a strange note. Umeko almost went to the phone to ask Miss Tanaka what it was all about, but she thought better of it. Miss Tanaka must have had a good reason to write as she had. Umeko would simply have to wait till next week to learn what had happened.

CHAPTER FOUR

やきいも
¥.10

ON THE DAY OF HER PIANO LESSON UMEKO HURRIED HOME from school and left the house again without even having a cup of tea.

"Won't you be hungry?" Umeko's mother asked.

"I'll stop by at the Potato Lady's," Umeko called back. Then, pulling on her boots, she ran out into the snow-covered yard.

The first snow of the year had fallen early that morning, and some of it still clung wet and heavy to the branches of the pine tree in the garden. The air was icy, and Umeko clapped her mittened hands together to keep them warm.

If it's this cold tomorrow, there'll be icicles glittering down from the roof, Umeko thought happily, and the stream beyond the forest will be ready for ice skating!

She kept these pleasant thoughts dancing through her head

and hurried toward the electric train station. When she turned onto the narrow shop-lined street, she caught the first tantalizing whiff of sweet potatoes sizzling in oil. Next to pancakes done to a golden brown over charcoal, Umeko thought fried sweet potatoes were just about the best thing anyone could have for three o'clock tea. Skirting bicycles and three-wheeled cars that plunged noisily down the cluttered street, Umeko hurried toward the shop of the old lady who sold the potatoes.

"Ah, here comes my best customer," called the Potato Lady with a friendly grin, and thrusting her long metal chopsticks into her pan of oil, she picked out the largest crisp golden slice she could find.

"I'm starved!" Umeko said, her mouth watering. "I just got home from school and came out again without even having any tea."

"Mah, mah," the old lady clucked sympathetically. "Then stay and eat your potato here, and I'll give you a cup of tea to go with it."

She wrapped Umeko's potato in a square of paper and reached for the small pot of tea that rested on the brazier behind her, but Umeko stopped her.

"Thanks just the same, but I'm late already," she explained. "I've got to get to my piano teacher's house by four o'clock."

Umeko hurried toward the station, nibbling stealthily at her steaming potato and hoping she wouldn't see anyone she knew. Mother would be horrified if she saw her eating a potato as she walked down the street.

Umeko always looked forward to going to Miss Tanaka's, for she would talk to her about the time she lived in England, or about literature or music, or even about politics and the role of women in Japan. She talked to Umeko as she would to another adult and seemed to understand her better than anyone else.

"Just be yourself," she had once said to Umeko, and with Miss Tanaka she always felt she could.

Umeko got off the train at Meguro Station and ran almost all the way to Miss Tanaka's house. It loomed large and tall behind a bamboo fence, looking as though it might have been picked up from England and suddenly transported to Japan. Umeko always felt that Miss Tanaka, with her graceful manner and sparkling smile, was exactly the right person to be living in that beautiful house.

When Umeko opened the gate and stepped into the garden, she saw Miss Tanaka standing over a small bonfire, prodding it with a long stick.

"Hello!" Miss Tanaka called, waving a gloved hand.

Umeko was surprised to see her bundled up in an old sweater and scarf. She was also wearing the baggy trousers that all women were being encouraged to wear as a uniform during wartime.

"You don't look right wearing those baggy old *mompei* and working in the yard," Umeko said, grinning. "I always think of you sitting at the piano in your blue silk dress and cashmere sweater."

Miss Tanaka threw back her head and laughed. "Ah, Umeko San, you incurable romanticist! I'm sorry to shatter your beautiful illusions about me, but, you know, I can be disgustingly practical when I want to be."

Umeko looked down at the pile of papers Miss Tanaka fed to the flames. "What in the world are you doing?" she asked.

"Just burning up some of my father's papers," she explained. "It may seem overapprehensive, but the military police would probably call these traitorous writings if they ever saw them, and I decided not to take any chances."

Umeko knew Miss Tanaka's father was an eminent scholar

of English literature and liberal in his thinking. He had spent many years in England and the United States, and before the war he had been outspoken in his criticism of the militarists.

"I suppose they think your father is a spy," Umeko said. "Have they searched your house yet?"

"They have, but, fortunately, these are some papers they missed." Miss Tanaka poked at the last bit of scorched paper and then turned to Umeko. "There, I think they're all burned," she said. "Let's go in and have some tea."

Tea at Miss Tanaka's meant black tea in thin Dresden cups, served with slivers of lemon and crumbly butter cookies. Umeko sat close to the warmth of the gas heater and forgot all about her sweet potato.

"Mmmmm," she murmured with her eyes half-closed. "This is the best three o'clock tea I've had in years!"

But now she remembered why she had been so eager to come. "Tell me why you told me not to bring my music," she said.

Miss Tanaka leaned back in her chair and smiled. "It's really a rather ridiculous story," she began. "A grim little policeman marched into our house last week and told me I must stop contaminating young minds with decadent Western music!"

"But how could he say such a stupid thing?" Umeko asked disbelievingly.

"He reminded me of the ban on Western music and said I was deliberately disobeying government regulations. Oh, he was terribly solemn and pompous," Miss Tanaka went on, and, imitating the little man, she puffed out her cheeks and wagged her head. "You can make things very difficult for your father," she mimicked gravely.

"But didn't you tell him you're not teaching jazz?" Umeko interrupted.

"Oh, I did, Umeko San, and I told him Beethoven and Chopin could hardly contaminate young minds, but nothing I said seemed to make a difference. The police are putting pressure on us, and there's no use making things any more difficult for my father."

"And so, no more piano lessons?" Umeko asked.

"I'm afraid not, Umeko San," Miss Tanaka answered. "The less reason we give the military police for coming here, the better."

Umeko sighed. "I guess both our fathers are just too dangerous!"

"Well, they've both been outspoken and honest about their beliefs, and naturally that has placed them in the public eye," Miss Tanaka explained.

Suddenly Umeko turned toward Miss Tanaka. "You know," she said, "some day I'd like to go off some place where no one will know who my father is. Then I'd curl my hair, and wear red dresses and jewelry, and maybe even become an actress or write a big fat novel."

Miss Tanaka's lips curved into a smile. "You sound exactly the way I did when I was your age," she said. "I know just how misunderstood you feel!"

Umeko was surprised. "But what did you ever have to complain about?" she asked. "You lived in England then and went to parties and wore pretty dresses."

"Oh, but there were many things I wasn't permitted to do," Miss Tanaka interrupted. "In fact, I remember a time when I wanted to run away from home and become a singer on the stage." Miss Tanaka laughed as she remembered.

"You did!" Umeko was amazed. "But I'll bet your father was never as strict as mine," she persisted. "I want to be me and not just his daughter all the time."

Miss Tanaka was silent as she poured Umeko another cup of tea. "Umeko San," she said slowly, "you mustn't be so impatient. There'll come a day when you will find that you can be your father's daughter and still be yourself. Then the two Umekos won't be pulling apart. They'll meet and become one. Some day, it will be a full circle," she said gently. "You'll see."

"I don't know," Umeko said doubtfully. Right now the two Umekos were moving in opposite directions. How could they ever meet?

"I'm sorry about our lessons," Miss Tanaka went on. "But do come to see me once in a while. Perhaps we could listen to records if we play them softly."

Umeko nodded. "I'll come," she said. "And even if I can't have lessons, I'll practice at home until the police come and make me stop."

"Just because you know you shouldn't?" Miss Tanaka asked smiling.

Umeko grinned. "I guess so," she admitted.

"All right then, you little rebel," Miss Tanaka said lightly. "But when you get caught, don't you dare tell them I'm your teacher!"

"Oh, I won't get caught," Umeko said confidently, and, as a matter of fact, she wasn't, for after her father had gone, the police seemed to lose interest in the Kagawas for the moment.

LIFE MOVED ALONG QUIETLY, AND THE COLD DARK DAYS OF WINTER were full of wind and snow. Umeko found it harder and harder to get up in the morning; and when she thought of the cold drafty classroom at school, she would slide down under her quilts, trying to soak up every bit of warmth she possibly could.

43

If she started for school early enough, she would have time to step inside at Kazu's, and sometimes Mrs. Takahashi would give her a cup of steaming tea. "*Sah, sah*," she would say cheerfully, "put a little warmth inside of you before you go." Then, as Umeko drank her tea, she would sometimes hear Kazu's father chanting the *sutra* before the family shrine, and the sweet smell of burning incense would come seeping through the paper doors.

"It won't be cold much longer," Mrs. Takahashi would say hopefully. "Soon the period of great cold will be over and then it will be spring."

"Spring according to the calendar only," Umeko would add with a shiver.

But Mrs. Takahashi shook her head. Like a good farmer's wife, she knew and anticipated every change in the weather. She would count the days until the vernal equinox when the trees would bud and the wheat grow tall. She would count the days till the rainy season in June and know that after the rains the heat of July would send the rice shooting up green and strong. And knowing that a sudden typhoon could destroy months of labor in a single day, she would watch anxiously for the passing of the two hundred tenth day, when the typhoon season was over and a safe harvest was assured.

"You wait," she said. "Soon we won't be begging for charcoal rations, and you'll be leaving your heavy coat at home."

And it was just as she said, for the snows of February melted away, the plum blossoms began to swell, and Umeko could feel the stirring of spring. Soon the rows of rape at the edge of the rice paddies burst into golden bloom and the cherry blossoms emerged in April like puffs of white smoke in a misty haze.

When the rice planting was over at Kazu's house, Umeko

knew the summer rainy season wasn't far behind. Soon June was upon them with an endless procession of dribbling, seeping rainy days. The war seemed as endless as the rain, and Toshio's letters were filled with a longing to be home. "Tell me what's happening back home," he urged in every letter, and Umeko wrote often, just as she had promised.

"Life's grown rather quiet at our house," she wrote. "In fact, people seem too busy with the war even to bother with ochugen this summer."

In past years, about mid-July, when the heat was unbearable and everyone was sipping cold drinks and eating shaved ice, Umeko remembered how friends had come calling with all sorts of ochugen gifts. This was the season when people in Japan said their thanks to those who had rendered kindnesses to them during the year, and in other years callers had streamed to the Kagawa house with gifts wrapped in silk furoshiki. They had brought baskets of juicy peaches and plums, bottles of fruit syrup, dried bonito, or even cans of cooking oil; the Kagawa kitchen had bulged with gifts from grateful friends.

"Not many people come to church any more, either," Umeko continued in her letter. "I suppose they're afraid of the military police. They're doing a good job of making life miserable, and we're all solemn and sober and dull as old razor blades! There'll be no fireworks along the river this year, of course, and I suppose they won't even want us to have firefly hunts.

"Anyway, we've sprouted our summer kimono and the house is airy and opened to the garden now, thanks to me," Umeko went on. "I took on your job of helping Hana San get out the bamboo screens and the mosquito netting, and now we sit on the veranda in the evenings and watch the moon come up over our wild green garden. Everything is enormous—even the spiders and their webs—and the trees are crawling with buzzing cicadas. If it weren't for the war, we'd probably hear the drums for the neighborhood Bon Festival dance. Oh me, will the war never end!" Umeko found she had ended on a note of complaint in spite of herself.

By the time the air grew clear and cool and the books and clothes that had grown moldy during the summer could be aired, it was again time for school. By now, many schools had begun to filter out much that was Western from their curriculum, emphasizing instead Japan's own history and culture. But at Keisen, English was still taught and chapel was still held every day. Umeko even saw and spoke to Americans from time to time, for several American missionaries had chosen to remain in Japan during the war. Most of them had been interned, but there were a few, like Mr. and Mrs. Topping, who were permitted to remain in their homes. Sometimes, when Mrs. Kagawa was able to get an extra ration of fish, or if someone from Hokkaido sent down some butter, she would send a little over to the Toppings with Umeko.

"Be careful, won't you?" she would caution, as Umeko left on her bicycle.

And Umeko would always call back, "I'm not afraid of those old military police. Just let them try to question me."

But one day when she had come to the Toppings with some butter, their maid ran into the living room, still carrying the broom with which she was sweeping the walk.

"They're coming again," she whispered hurriedly.

"The military police?" Mrs. Topping asked quietly.

The maid nodded. "I think Umeko San had better leave quickly."

"Use the back door," Mrs. Topping said, and she hurried Umeko outside. Umeko put on her shoes but didn't even bother to tie the laces. Then suddenly she remembered. "My bicycle's out in front!" she said frantically. "How can I get my bicycle?"

But it was too late. Umeko could already hear the police rapping at the front entrance. "You'll just have to come back for it another time, Umeko San," Mrs. Topping said as she hurried to the front door.

Umeko darted out to the back road and looked at the long stretch ahead of her. It would take nearly a half hour if she walked home, and then she'd have to come back again for her bicycle. Umeko wondered if she dared go to the front entrance and sneak away with the bicycle while the police were inside. Her heart thumped at the thought of being pulled inside and questioned. But after all, she thought, what's so terrible about bringing two old friends a little butter? I'm going to do it, she decided, and, taking a deep breath, she walked around the high wooden fence to the front gate. The police had left their own bicycles just inside the gate, but Umeko's was farther inside beside the cedar tree.

Umeko slid open the front gate quietly and looked in. The front door of the house was closed. If only they would stay inside till she was safely out the gate. Umeko held her breath and tiptoed up the gravel walk. Suppose they should hear the crunching of her footsteps! She got to her bicycle, wheeled it around, and almost crashed it into the tree in her hurry to get out. She ran quickly to the gate, pushed out her bike, and hopped on without stopping to close the gate behind her. Umeko pedaled as fast as she could, not daring to look back for fear she might see two policemen pedaling behind her.

When, at last, she got home, she could scarcely speak. "Mother!" she puffed, "I almost got caught today."

"Who was trying to catch you?" It was a man's voice.

The voice sounded like her father's, but how could it be? Umeko ran to the study, looked in, and there he was, sitting at his desk as though he had never been away. "Who was trying to catch you?" he asked again.

But Umeko was so full of her own questions, she didn't even listen to him. "Father, what are you doing back home? Are you sick?" she asked. "Is the war over? What has happened? Will you stay now?"

Father smiled. "You haven't changed a bit, have you, Ume Chan?" he said.

Father spoke slowly. "The navy wants the island of Teshima evacuated," he explained. "It was necessary for us all to leave —the farmers, the orphans, even the T.B. patients."

"Then you're home to stay?" Umeko asked again.

Father shook his head. "I hope so, but I don't know. I just don't know." And it was only then that Umeko noticed how tired he seemed.

Although Father was back, he worked quietly at home, seeing only a few of his close friends who came to call. And in his room, Umeko knew that he kept a bag packed so he could leave at a moment's notice.

It had been a long time now since the victory parades had gone weaving down the streets. In fact, people were beginning to wonder what had become of Japan's great Imperial Navy, but no one dared ask aloud, and everyone lived each day in questioning doubt.

"We haven't heard from my brother for a whole month," Kazu said one day. Umeko nodded sympathetically. "Toshio's letters have stopped coming, too."

The war seemed to weigh down on the tiny islands like a great unwieldly burden too heavy to bear, and the nation's leaders now prodded and urged its people to sacrifice even more. Men up to sixty and women up to forty were being drafted for work in factories, and one day Umeko learned that now students, too, would be expected to do their share.

"From now on, you will work six days a week in a factory and report to school for classes one day only," the teacher announced. "You will receive twenty-five yen a month for this work, and we'll be able to tell you in a few days where you will be sent."

"It sounded as though we'd be sent away somewhere, didn't it?" Umeko said to Kazu as they walked home.

Kazu nodded. "It did sound that way."

"But think what that means!" Umeko continued. "We'll leave home and probably live together in a dormitory somewhere. Won't that be wonderful?"

"It would be fun," Kazu agreed, "but I'm worried about school. If we have classes only once a week, we're going to get awfully far behind. I mean, we'll never be ready to take college entrance exams when the war's over."

But Umeko was not concerned. "Just think," she went on enthusiastically, "we'll actually be taking part in the war effort and we'll be earning our own spending money besides!"

It was a tantalizing thought, and Umeko went straight to her room when she got home. She sat down at her desk and made a list of the things she'd want to take with her.

"Mittens, wool scarf, diary, stationery and stamps, red camellia pin, red sweater . . ." the list went on and on. When she had finished, she wrote letters to her sister, now in Nagano-ken, where her school had moved, to her brother at the university in Chiba, and to Toshio somewhere out in the Pacific.

"At last, I feel really grown up," she wrote cheerfully. "I'll actually be doing something for our country. I'll be earning money, and I'll be living away from home for the first time!"

ᴇᴀᴄʜ ᴅᴀʏ ᴀᴛ sᴄʜᴏᴏʟ, ᴛʜᴇ ɢɪʀʟs ᴄʀᴏᴡᴅᴇᴅ ᴀʀᴏᴜɴᴅ ᴛʜᴇɪʀ teacher. "Haven't we been assigned to a factory yet?" they asked impatiently.

And each day the teacher would shake her head. "Not yet. I'll let you know as soon as we hear."

In the meantime Umeko continued to empty her drawers and plan her packing, feeling already the faint glow of independence. "I'll write often," she promised her mother. "You won't have to worry about me."

At last one morning the teacher smiled. "We've finally had word," she said. "You girls have been assigned to work at the Fujioka Light Arms factory."

"The one down the road?" someone asked. The teacher nodded. "You girls are fortunate," she continued. "You will be able to live at home, report to school as usual, and go to the factory from here each morning." She went on giving the hours and details of the work, but Umeko no longer listened.

"Then we won't be living together in dormitories at all?" she interrupted.

"No, you'll be living right at home," the teacher repeated, "and you'll begin work tomorrow morning."

Umeko slumped back in her chair, feeling miserably cheated. Why, half the joy of going to work had been the thought of living away from home with the other girls. She wished she hadn't bragged to Toshio and her brother and sister. Now I'll have to tell them we're being kept home close to our mamas after all, she thought dismally. When she got home she quickly threw everything back in her drawers before anyone could discover how silly she had been. Going to work wasn't going to be so interesting after all.

The next morning Umeko's class gathered at school and then marched down the road to the factory together. They were ushered into the sitting room outside the factory manager's office and told to be seated on a row of stiff folding chairs. Soon the manager strode in with a brisk military air, his face solemn, his eyes twitching with nervousness.

"Good morning," he said with a slight bow. "We are pleased that you young ladies are joining in the great war effort of our beloved country. I am sure you must feel very proud."

The girls nodded, and the man went on in a shrill, high voice, telling them of the importance of their work in bringing about the Greater East Asia Co-Prosperity Sphere. When he had finished, the girls felt like soldiers about to plunge into battle, and for a moment Umeko wondered if they wouldn't suddenly break out in a shout of "*Banzai*."

A supervisor appeared from the side door and announced

that she would direct the girls into the factory proper. She looked to be about forty and, like the girls, wore baggy *mompei* and a faded sweater beneath her loose jacket.

"Now," she said in a low raspy voice, "please watch carefully." She held up a wooden frame strung with rows of thin wire. "Your job is to tie aluminum parts onto these wires. When the frame is filled, it will be taken to a vat and placed in a solution that will prevent the parts from rusting. You must be sure the parts are tied on securely. Is that clear?"

The girls nodded and waited until the woman had finished a violent fit of coughing. She covered her face with a big handkerchief and turned away.

"It sounds as if she has tuberculosis," Kazu whispered to Umeko.

"We may all get T.B. if we have to work in this drafty old factory very long," Umeko answered darkly.

But now the woman had stopped coughing. Her face was flushed, and her lips were dry. "Take your places at the tables, please," she said with difficulty. "We will get to work now."

As Umeko began she thought of the soldiers who would some day use the arms this factory produced. Even Toshio or Kazu's brother might use them one day, and their very lives might depend on their effectiveness. Suddenly Umeko was filled with a sense of mission, and she worked without a moment's rest until the factory whistle startled her with its shrill blast.

"Lunch time already!" she said as she stretched. "The day certainly goes quickly when you're busy."

But Tomi, who worked next to her, began to laugh. "Not that quickly," she said. "That was only the ten o'clock whistle. We get five minutes' rest now."

By five o'clock, Umeko felt as though every bone in her

body ached. "I don't see how I'll ever make it home," she sighed as she collapsed at the entrance of Kazu's house.

But Kazu only laughed at her. "Some day you should try bending over a wet paddy, planting rice all day," she said. "Then you'd discover what hard work really is!"

When Umeko got home, her mother sighed sympathetically. "You'll soon grow used to it, and then it won't seem so hard," she said, and, using a precious ration of fuel, she built a fire for a bath that night. Umeko sank into the steaming hot water, and, as she soaked in the big wooden tub with the water up to her neck, she finally felt as though she might survive another day at the factory.

It was just as Mother said, however. The work grew easier as the days went by, and soon Umeko could look forward to the twenty-five yen she earned each month.

"We're really becoming independent," she would say happily to Kazu as they thought of ways in which they might spend the money. And Kazu would agree. "It is nice, isn't it? Even though the stores are empty and there isn't much to buy."

The first big air raid over Tokyo came one day while Umeko was at the factory. The sirens began to scream and the voice over the loudspeaker was tense. "The B-29's have reached Mount Fuji. They are heading toward Tokyo. Tokyo may be the target city . . . Tokyo may be the target city," the voice warned urgently.

The girls grabbed their quilted hoods and their emergency rations and ran to the underground shelter. Umeko and Kazu and about ten other girls were assigned to a small shelter in the far corner of the factory grounds. There they huddled in the darkness, scarcely breathing, straining to hear the drone of the first formation of planes.

"Here they come," someone whispered. No one moved. Each of them felt that even the slightest movement or sound would be spotted by the gunners on the terrible planes that droned by overhead. It sounded as though thousands of planes were sweeping across the skies, and Umeko almost wished she could see such an awesome sight.

"They seem to be heading for the center of Tokyo," Tomi whispered. "I hope they don't get our house."

Soon Umeko could hear the dull thud of explosions that shook even their small shelter far out on the outskirts of the city. Bits of dirt filtered down around them, and for a dreadful moment Umeko wondered what would happen if their shelter should collapse with them inside. It seemed hours as they sat waiting for the all clear. At last, the explosions stopped, there was a long eerie silence, and then the sirens blared the all clear. When they stepped out of the shelter, gray smoke billowed above Tokyo like a writhing monster, and here and there the glow of flames still lit up the sky. The acrid smell of smoke soon drifted toward them on the wind, and bits of ash swirled high in the sky overhead.

Umeko shuddered. "I hope we don't have any more raids like this," she said as they walked back to the factory. But all the girls knew there would be more and that perhaps, some day, the bombs might fall on the factory where they worked.

Almost every day after that the sirens wailed, and the girls spent more and more time inside the shelter. But strangely enough, as the air raids increased, they began to feel immune from danger. If they had been safe all this time, they felt they would somehow be safe always. And now, as they sat in their shelter, they relaxed and nibbled the soybeans in their emergency rations and talked about many things. They talked about the war and the soldiers to whom they sent letters and about all the delicious things they would eat when the war was over. They solved the problems of Japan and the world in the darkness of their small shelter, and then, often, they drifted to talk about love and marriage and the role of women in Japan. Here they lingered long and lovingly, for it was a subject close to their hearts.

"I think arranged marriages are horrible," Umeko said one day. "Why should a girl have to marry a man she scarcely knows?"

"But, Umeko San," Tomi argued, "someone has to arrange a meeting. We'd never find anyone by ourselves."

"That's just the trouble," Umeko answered. "If we had the chance to go out and get to know more men, we wouldn't have to have go-betweens. We could choose for ourselves."

"But you might not find as nice a match," Kazu ventured. "You know, it's hard to find just the right person from a good family, with a good job and good schooling."

Umeko shrugged. "But, at least, you could marry someone you really loved," she said.

When the question of love arose, someone invariably asked, "Well then, suppose you could marry a poor clerk you loved or an up-and-coming banker you didn't love but who could give you a good secure life. Which would you choose?"

Tomi was always quick to answer. "I'd choose the banker, of course," she'd say. "After all, you'd have a much better life, and besides, Mother always says that love comes later."

"That's what my mother says, too," Kazu would murmur, "but still, if I could really choose, I think I'd rather have someone I loved. I don't mind being poor. I think I'd rather be happy." But even as she spoke, Kazu grew solemn. It was as though she knew that for her this could never be more than a dim, hopeful dream.

Umeko rested her chin on her palms and listened to them talk. "What about you?" Tomi would ask her.

"Oh, me?" Umeko would say. "I think I'll arrange to fall in love with a rich banker. That would solve everything, wouldn't it?"

"That would be a pretty clever stunt, all right," Tomi would say with a grin. "But I'll bet you can't do it. Life just isn't that simple."

"I'll say it isn't," Umeko had to agree, and they would discover that they still hadn't solved their biggest problem.

Still it was better to sit in the cozy darkness and talk than to go on with the tedious work in the factory. "I don't think I can bear to tie on another part," Umeko would say each morning, and, as winter came and the days grew bitterly cold, the work grew more and more unbearable. Soon the girls found they would have to stop every once in a while and blow on their fingers and stamp their feet, just to keep them from growing numb.

"Those lucky girls who work in the laundry," Umeko murmured to Kazu.

"Why? They don't have any heat either, do they?" Kazu asked. "I thought all the metal heaters had been turned in."

"No, of course, they don't have heaters," Umeko explained, "but when the supervisor isn't looking, they stop ironing those army shirts and run the irons over each other. They say the heat comes through just right over their coats and sweaters!"

As the days and months wore on, there were fewer and fewer aluminum parts to work with, and some days all they did was straighten the wires on the empty racks, getting them ready for parts that never came.

"This is worse than having too much to do," the girls complained, for now the monotony of each day loomed larger than ever before. Gradually, they saw less and less of the supervisor with the cough, and finally she didn't appear at all.

"I hear her house burned down in the last raid," Tomi said. "Maybe she was killed." But others said she had died of tuberculosis because she hadn't been able to get any medicine. Whatever the reason, she had stopped coming altogether, and now the girls worked mostly on their own.

One day Tomi approached Umeko and whispered in her ear. "Want to sneak out early next Wednesday and go to a concert?"

"Would I?" Umeko almost shouted. "I haven't been to a concert since Tanaka San stopped teaching piano. Can Kazu go, too?"

Tomi nodded. "Sure, but we'd better not ask any others. If too many of us sneak out together, someone might notice."

And so it was decided that the following Wednesday they would go outside with everyone for the three o'clock rest period and not come back. Kazu was a little wary. "Do you really think it's all right?" she asked again and again.

But Umeko couldn't conceal her enthusiasm. "Of course, it's all right," she said. "We're not really doing anything wrong. There's no work for us in the factory, anyway, and lots of girls have been leaving early."

It was so simple to stroll out of the gate when the watchman was looking the other way, Umeko felt disappointed. "Well, our little escape wasn't very exciting, was it?" she said glumly, as they boarded the crowded train for downtown Tokyo. But the desolation of the city quickly shocked her from such thoughts. Tokyo had become a shambles of gutted buildings and piles of rubble. Only a few concrete buildings stood here and there like lonely sentinels, and the homeless were wandering about the streets looking dazed and frightened and lost. Umeko couldn't bear to look at them.

Tomi led the way to a small two-story building. "It's just a string quartet," she murmured. "They're all students, but they're good. I know the violinist. I hope the police won't stop them today."

Soon they were sitting in a small crowded hall listening avidly to the music of Mozart and Handel and Bach, and, as Umeko listened, she forgot about the factory and the cold and even about the war itself. It was like being transported into a separate and far-off world.

"I'd forgotten what it was like to listen to such beautiful music," Kazu sighed softly when it was over. "Why does the world have to be full of fighting and bombs and death when it could be so full of wonderful things?"

"It's because of those stupid militarists who got us into this war," Umeko said bitterly.

But Tomi quickly silenced her. "You'd better not talk like that in public," she warned. "You never know who might be listening."

The three walked back to the station in silence and when they got to Kanda, Tomi left them, saying she wanted to stop to see her aunt. Umeko thought of Miss Tanaka as they neared Meguro Station. She would have enjoyed the concert so much. The train had just pulled into Meguro when suddenly the air raid sirens began to wail. "Air raid!" the people shouted, and as the doors slid open, they pushed and shoved in their attempt to get to the nearest shelter.

"Oh, Umeko, what shall we do?" Kazu moaned.

"Let's try to get to Tanaka San's," Umeko shouted. "I'd rather be in her shelter than in this public one."

She grabbed Kazu's hand, and they ran across the street toward Miss Tanaka's house. But they had gone only a few steps when a policeman stopped them. "Here!" he shouted. "Didn't you hear the siren? Get into that shelter!" And without another word he pushed them back toward the station.

"We're going to a friend's house. It's just a little way from here. Please let us go!" Umeko pleaded.

But the policeman took them firmly by their arms and led them to the shelter. "Quickly! Inside!" he said, and Kazu and Umeko soon found themselves in the crowded darkness with what seemed like hundreds of people. They clung to each other in the dim, stuffy shelter and waited for the sound of the planes. Somehow there seemed to be an ominous air about the shelter, and Umeko had the terrible feeling that today their luck might run out. Suppose they were killed! No one would ever find them, for she hadn't told her mother where she was going, only that she would be late. That's what I get for doing something I shouldn't, Umeko thought gloomily, but it was too late now.

The planes were overhead now, and the shelter was silent except for the sound of children crying and being comforted. The droning went on. If only the planes would go by. And then, suddenly, there was an explosion that seemed to rip the shelter apart. Umeko closed her eyes tight and prayed that they might somehow be saved. For a moment she was sure the shelter had had a direct hit, but soon she heard voices around her murmuring, "That was a close one!" and she knew they were still safe.

Everyone in the shelter seemed to be edging toward the exit. There was the terrible fear of being buried underground and everyone was determined to leave the minute the all clear sounded. It was as though the whole shelter was poised for the big push to get outside, and when, at last, the all clear did blow, the crowd crashed down on Umeko and Kazu in a mad stampede. Umeko found herself being pushed out with the crowd, but Kazu was pushed back. "Help! Umeko!" She could hear Kazu's voice, but she couldn't even turn to look back. The people pushed and shoved and stumbled out, and when, at last, Kazu emerged, she was limping and her face was twisted with pain.

"I fell. . . . My ankle. . . , " she murmured, and then she slumped to the ground. Umeko dragged her to a clearing and rubbed her hands and wrists. "Kazu!" she shouted. If only I could get some water, she thought frantically. If I could just get to Tanaka San.

Umeko looked around for help, but all the people were rushing to see if their houses were still standing. The smell of smoke was strong in the air, and Umeko felt as though she would choke.

"Please help me!" she called to people who hurried by, but no one seemed to hear her. At last, Umeko knew that she would have to carry Kazu to Miss Tanaka's alone. Kazu was conscious now but in such pain she couldn't even limp.

"Don't worry," Umeko repeated again and again, and pulling Kazu's arms across her chest, she hoisted her on her own back. Somehow Umeko found the strength to carry Kazu to Miss Tanaka's house and there, panting and half-crying, she pounded on the door. The house was strangely dark and quiet, and it was only after Umeko shouted and called several times that she heard footsteps in the hall.

"Who is it?" Miss Tanaka called.

"It's Umeko. Help me, please!"

"Ah," Miss Tanaka sounded relieved. She unlocked the door quickly and then seeing Kazu she asked, "What in the world happened?"

60

Slipping Kazu from her back, Umeko poured out her story all at once—the concert, the air raid, Kazu's ankle. "I'm afraid her ankle's broken," she finished. She could see now that the ankle was swollen to twice its size.

Miss Tanaka didn't waste a moment. "Phone your mothers and tell them you're here and safe," she said. "I'll get the doctor down the street."

It was only after the doctor had said Kazu's ankle was only sprained and had taped it up for her that Umeko noticed Miss Tanaka was acting strangely. She had never seen her so nervous and upset. Her parents, too, seemed terribly uneasy.

When the doctor left after giving Kazu a precious aspirin tablet, Umeko asked Miss Tanaka if something was wrong.

"Well, as a matter of fact, yes," Miss Tanaka admitted nervously. "We've been warned that the military police are rounding up people on their suspect list today, and at the moment we're waiting for a friend who will drive my father to his summer villa in the mountains." Miss Tanaka glanced at her watch. "He's due any minute. I do wish he'd hurry or the police may get here first."

Miss Tanaka's father looked at Umeko and Kazu. "You girls had better come along with me," he suggested. "I'm sure Kazu can't manage the train with that ankle, and we can easily drop you off on the way."

"Maybe you'd better not go to my house," Umeko answered. "The police may be there, too. I'll get off at Kazu's."

Miss Tanaka brought their shoes around to the back entrance. "You may have to leave in a hurry," she warned, and at that very moment there was a light knock at the back door.

"He's here," Professor Tanaka whispered, and picking up his bag, he hurried out the back way.

Miss Tanaka pushed Umeko and Kazu after him. "Hurry!" she urged.

As she helped Kazu out of the back door, Umeko could hear someone banging on the front gate. "Tanaka San! Open the door! Military police!" Umeko and Kazu plunged into the waiting car, and the driver sped away down the dark back alley, avoiding the street out front. Professor Tanaka explained to his friend why the girls had come along, and they were soon speeding toward Kazu's house. They rode through the dark streets in tense, anxious silence, and when they reached the Takahashi house, Umeko got out with Kazu. "Thank you so much," she said quickly to Professor Tanaka. "Good-by! Good luck!" The professor waved briefly, and then the car disappeared in the blackness of the night.

When Umeko hurried home, she found Hana in the kitchen trembling with fright. Her mother sat alone in her father's study looking pale and tired.

"Ah, Ume Chan, it was a good thing you were away today," she sighed. "The military police were everywhere."

"Did they take Father?" Umeko asked quickly.

"No, we were fortunate," her mother continued. "Friends came to warn us in time, and before they got here he left for Akagi Village to be with the Suzukis."

"Just like Professor Tanaka," Umeko broke in, and she poured out her own story of all that had happened to her, to Kazu, and to Professor Tanaka.

Her mother shook her head as she listened. "*Mah, mah,* such a dangerous thing," she said. "You could have been killed in that shelter—and Kazu Chan with you. And leaving the factory early was a shameful thing to do."

"I know," Umeko said, "I've had my punishment!" And as she ate the steamed potato Hana had saved for her supper, she smiled to think how disappointed she'd been when she left the factory because there hadn't been enough excitement. I've had enough excitement today to last me the rest of the year, she thought wearily.

But when she heard Hana talking to Mother in a low anxious whisper, she wondered if perhaps this wasn't just the beginning.

"It makes me tremble each time I think how close Sensei came to being killed," Hana said to Mother. "Imagine, those militarists wanting to assassinate Kagawa Sensei!"

"I can't believe they really would have killed him," Umeko's mother answered, "and, yet, there's talk that they fear we Christians will help the Americans when they invade Japan."

Umeko's head began to whirl. Assassination! Americans invading Japan! What ever was going to become of them all? And what would happen to Father? The heavy weight of fear seemed to engulf Umeko, but she couldn't even find the strength to think properly. She was tired right down to her toes.

If I could just take a hot bath and have some steaming rice and bean soup, she thought wistfully. But Umeko knew this was an impossible dream and that, once more, she would go to bed tired and hungry and cold.

CHAPTER SIX

IT ALL HAPPENED AS IF MR. SUZUKI KNEW JUST HOW HUNGRY Umeko was. A few days later a letter came from him inviting Umeko and her mother to visit them in Akagi Village.

"It will be nice for you to see Dr. Kagawa's new wartime home," he wrote. "We would also like to show you what we are doing here, and perhaps you'd like to take home some of the carrots and turnips we've grown in our fields."

Umeko whooped with joy. "Perhaps!" she shouted. "Let him just try to send us home without some food." She felt dizzy just thinking of having something else to eat besides potatoes and potato leaves.

As soon as church services were over on Sunday, Umeko and her mother went to Ueno Station to catch the train for Akagi Village. Umeko groaned as she saw the crowds on the platform. Everyone was carrying knapsacks or *furoshiki* or big rucksacks. Everyone was going to the country for exactly the same purpose.

"All of Tokyo must be going out to beg food from the farmers today," Umeko said, shaking her head as she looked around. "No wonder everyone said the farmers were getting rich."

Umeko heard a woman complaining behind her. "I can't stand the thought of groveling before those haughty farmers again," she said bitterly. "The way they carry on, you'd think we were asking them for free food."

"I'm taking up my last good kimono today," her friend answered sadly. "Who would ever have dreamed that I'd be trading my wedding kimono for a few pounds of potatoes!"

As their train approached, the people pushed closer to the edge of the platform. No one wanted to be left behind, and, yet, there didn't seem to be enough room for everyone. Some people pushed their way right through the open windows, clambering in where the glass had been blown away or broken.

"Be careful," Umeko's mother cautioned.

But already Umeko could feel the grip of her mother's hand slipping, and, as the weight of the crowd pushed her into the train, she saw that her mother was being left behind in the corridor of the car. "Mother!" Umeko called, but she was pushed farther and farther up the aisle. There was no getting together now.

Slowly, the train began to move, as people still climbed in through every open window. Arms and legs seemed to be flinging about wildly, and Umeko could no longer see her mother at all. She tried to turn, but she couldn't even move. Her right hand was pinned against her chest, still clutching her empty rucksack, and she discovered that she couldn't even raise her left hand to scratch the tip of her nose.

The train sped out beyond the charred ruins of Tokyo, past fields of sun-soaked wheat, stopping at every little station it passed. At each stop the train deposited a few people who would then trudge slowly to the friend or relative who might sell them a little food.

At last, Umeko found that she could raise her hand to scratch her nose and, turning, she could just see the top of Mother's head. It was not much farther to Akagi Village. Umeko decided she'd better edge her way toward the exit, but she hadn't gone more than a few inches when the train slowed down.

"Akagi Village! Akagi Village!" a conductor's shrill voice drifted in from the platform outside. Umeko pushed with all her strength as she tried to move toward the door, but no one could seem to give way at all.

"Please! I must get off!" Umeko shouted. "Let me through, please!" But the harder she pushed the less progress she made. The conductor was already blowing his whistle for the train to start. Umeko looked frantically out the window and saw her mother standing on the platform, waiting for her. Mrs. Kagawa's eyes suddenly swept back across the car, and she saw Umeko still struggling in the middle of the car.

"Use the window, Ume Chan!" her mother called to her. "Use the window!"

Umeko lunged toward the nearest window, stepping on toes and stumbling over laps. The people sitting near an open window helped push her out, and, with Mother pulling from the outside, she somehow managed to crawl out head first. Her feet touched the station platform just as the train began to move.

"Mah! Are you all right?" her mother asked anxiously.

"I don't know!" Umeko groaned, "I feel as though every bone in my body is squashed flat!"

"I was so worried," Mrs. Kagawa said, "I was afraid you'd never get out!"

"I was, too," Umeko sighed. "I thought I'd surely end up in Sendai before I could get out of that miserable train!"

Just then a familiar voice called to them. It was Mr. Suzuki, smiling and clopping noisily toward them in his wooden geta.

"Ah, how good it is to see you again, Suzuki San," Mother said. She bowed and smiled and grasped Mr. Suzuki's hand.

"And it is so good to see you again," he said warmly. "We have thought of you often. And, Umeko San, I hear you're working in a factory now."

Umeko nodded. "I thought that was hard work," she said laughingly, "but it's nothing compared to what we went through on the train to get here."

"Ah, I know," Mr. Suzuki sympathized. "I've heard how great the crowds are on the trains these days. But come," he added, quickly. "You will feel better when you have rested and had some tea."

He led them out to the narrow dirt road that stretched between the fields of wheat. Mr. Suzuki shook his head as he looked at the crops. "The farmers work hard, but the soil is so poor that the crops are never good enough to enable them to pay off their debts."

As he spoke, a woman approached them on the road. She was not old and yet she was bent almost double from the burden of faggots strapped to her back.

"Ah, Sensei," she smiled, bobbing her head in a series of little bows.

Mr. Suzuki smiled. "You're feeling better?" he asked.

"Not better, but not worse either," the woman answered. "I have no time to waste on being sick," and, bowing once again, she trudged off down the road.

"I suppose she is overworked like most farm wives," Mrs. Kagawa said, looking after the small pathetic figure with its heavy load.

Mr. Suzuki nodded. "She's probably been up since five o'clock this morning, washing and cooking and then working in the fields," he said slowly. "And when she's fed her family and put the children to bed, she'll mend and sew and be the last to go to bed."

Umeko sighed. "I'll never be a farmer's wife for sure," she said firmly. "That's a horrible way to have to live."

"But as busy as they are," Mr. Suzuki went on wonderingly, "they have found time to come to classes—mothers with infants tied to their backs, young girls who haven't been able to finish school, even some old grandmothers." He told them how he and Mrs. Suzuki farmed during the day and at night helped the village women improve their reading and writing.

But now, as they passed a bamboo thicket and turned a bend in the road, Mr. Suzuki paused and looked up. "Well," he said, "I've talked so much, we are home already." He pointed to the crest of a small hill. "There is our home," he said.

Umeko led the way, bounding up the sharp path toward the thatch-roofed house.

"Hello! Here we are!" she shouted, poking her head inside the doorway.

Immediately, she heard footsteps pattering toward the entrance. Mrs. Suzuki knelt to the floor as she bowed to greet Umeko and her mother.

"*Mah, mah,* it is so very good to have you come," she said, and, as she grasped her outstretched hand, Umeko was startled by the calluses that covered the palm.

"Please come in," said Mrs. Suzuki quickly, her sun-browned face wrinkled in a smile. "*Sensei* is in the sitting room."

Umeko found her father reading the Bible, using his magnifying glass as usual, to aid his weakened eyes. He seemed surprised as he looked up and saw Umeko.

"Did you forget we were coming today, Father?" Umeko asked with a grin. She knew this wasn't entirely impossible, for when Father was reading, he never knew what was going on around him.

Dr. Kagawa rose and returned her grin, saying, "I was absorbed in the book," he answered, "but I could hardly forget your visit, Ume Chan. The Suzukis and I have talked of nothing else all week."

Mrs. Suzuki hurried out for some tea, and Dr. Kagawa walked to the veranda and slid open the glass doors. As they looked out they could see terraced fields stretching down to the railroad and up again on the hills beyond. High in the cold blue sky, the hawks were wheeling and scolding at the strips of tinfoil that glittered in the sun and frightened them away from the fields.

Umeko's father sighed as he surveyed the peaceful scene.

"If I could only share the peace of this village with all our people," he said thoughtfully.

"Ah, but you'll soon be sharing your knowledge with all our villagers," Mr. Suzuki consoled him. "It will be wonderful to have a gospel school for our boys and girls."

"And we must help the farmers improve their techniques of cultivating the land," Dr. Kagawa added with enthusiasm. "We must teach them to plant trees on the mountainsides and raise goats for milk."

"And encourage them to form a cooperative, too," Mrs. Kagawa added.

"Yes, yes, of course."

Umeko could see the color flow back into her father's face

69

as he spoke. He was always happiest when he was making plans such as these to help the farmers and laborers.

Mrs. Suzuki had now returned with the tea, and she spoke eagerly of her sewing class for young girls and the community center they hoped to start for the young boys.

"It makes my heart heavy," Mrs. Kagawa added with a troubled expression, "to think there are so many other villages like this that need help."

Umeko sat back and listened quietly. It was as though they had forgotten that she was there. She had planned to tell the Suzukis all about the cold unheated factory, to show them the chilblains on her hands from working without gloves, to tell them how there was no more fuel and how they now had to go to the public baths. She especially wanted to tell them how they had eaten potatoes and potato leaves until they were ready to sprout them from their ears. But, somehow, there seemed no room in this conversation for such complaints, and Umeko found herself listening quietly.

The sun had already dipped down behind the blue-gray hills when Mrs. Suzuki served them a simple supper, using the rice she had carefully set aside for the occasion.

"Eat plenty, Umeko Chan," Mrs. Suzuki urged. "It's a little easier for us to get rice out here in the country."

Those were the sweetest words Umeko had heard in a long time. And as she ate she sighed, "Now I can die happy, even if a bomb should fall on me tomorrow!"

When Umeko and her mother were ready to leave for home, the Suzukis filled their rucksacks with potatoes, turnips, and even a little rice. Umeko felt as though she were carrying a pack of precious jewels on her back, and she smiled to herself at the thought that she must look exactly like the stooped woman they had met on the road that afternoon.

"You must come again," the Suzukis urged.

"We will," both Umeko and her mother promised, and once again they were back on a crowded train headed for Tokyo.

Again, it was impossible for them to stay together, and Umeko found herself jammed against the side of one of the seats. She leaned wearily against it, sorting out the thoughts that tumbled about in her mind. Somehow, she couldn't forget the earnestness with which her parents and the Suzukis had talked about helping the villagers. Each of them had devoted his entire life to the service of others. She thought especially about her mother and father—how they had gone to live in the slums of Shinkawa in Kobe to care for the sick and the unloved and to teach them of Christ's love.

It was surely a noble way of life, and, caught up in a brief fire of inspiration, Umeko thought of giving up her own selfish dreams for such a life of service. But almost as quickly she knew she could not easily discard her dreams.

"Why shouldn't I live my own life and have a good time?" she said to herself. "Mother and Father do enough for other people. I'm going to enjoy life and be good to myself. I'm selfish," and she shrugged as she added, "but I just can't help it."

Umeko had been so busy with her thoughts, she hardly noticed that they had already come into Ueno Station. But as she moved out, pushed by the crowds, she knew something was wrong, for now she could stand up straight. The weight of her rucksack had suddenly vanished, and as the full realization of the horrible discovery struck her, Umeko found her mother.

"Oh, Mother," she wailed. "Someone slit a hole in my bag and stole all my vegetables. How could anyone be so mean?"

"That's too bad," her mother consoled, "but everyone is just as hungry as you are. You've just got to feel that you shared a few meals with someone else and forget it. It can't be helped."

Umeko felt her mother's bag. "No one slit yours?" she asked. Mother shook her head. "No, mine is still quite full and heavy," she answered.

It's as though the thief knew, Umeko thought. I am the selfish one and Mother is not.

It was now 1945, four years since Pearl Harbor and the beginning of the war, and Umeko was sixteen. The air raids over Tokyo gradually grew more and more severe, and there were days when Umeko felt as though she spent more time in the shelter than in the outside world. Now they slept with their clothes on, ready to run to the shelter in their yard the moment the sirens sounded. Sometimes, when Umeko heard the sirens in the middle of the night, she would be so hopelessly sleepy that she would simply slip down further between her quilt and cover her ears, murmuring, "I just don't care if I'm hit." But soon her mother or Hana would be there, shaking her and dragging her down the stairs into the damp chill of the underground shelter.

Then, there came the terrible raid when all Tokyo was ablaze, when hundreds and thousands of people were killed, and when the city struggled and smothered in the blackness of smoke and fire for three long days. The roads near the home of the Kagawas were clogged with refugees escaping to the countryside. They fled the flames with only a bundle of clothing or a bucket, a bag of potatoes, or whatever they had been able to salvage before their houses were devoured by the flames. Mothers carried wailing babies on their backs or pulled them along in carts filled with silent, frightened children.

Before long, flimsy wooden shacks began to spring up in the forest where Umeko had gone so often to play. Here people crowded together, living like frightened animals, eating grass and leaves. They lived with the sun and wind and rain that sifted in through the walls, praying that the bombs wouldn't follow them to the outskirts of the city. Umeko tried not to pass too close to their shacks, for it frightened her to look at the eyes of those who lived there. They were the staring eyes of people who had seen horrible things, and they made Umeko shudder.

More and more, families in the neighborhood were receiving the small white box that contained the ashes of a soldier who had died in battle. And one day Kazu came to see Umeko, with eyes red and swollen from weeping.

"My brother has come home to his final rest," she said tearfully. "He went off so bravely and cheerfully, and now all we have of him is the small white box."

When Umeko and her mother went to express their sympathy, Kazu's father spoke deliberately. "He died for his country," he said almost fiercely. "We are proud of him." But Kazu's mother was silent and grim. She sat with her head bowed low, too full of grief even to shed a tear.

Umeko wondered if one day her family might get a small white box. It had been so long since she had heard from Toshio, perhaps he, too, was dead somewhere. But this was an ugly thought, and whenever it occurred, Umeko shook it away quickly.

When at last the people of Japan thought they could bear no more, when it seemed almost better to die than to struggle so hard to keep alive, there came news of the strange bombs that had demolished Hiroshima and Nagasaki. A single bomb over each city, and yet thousands had died. It was a strange phenomenon that no one could explain.

Shortly after, the girls were told to report to school one day instead of to the factory. There was to be a special broadcast on the radio, and it was rumored that the Emperor himself would speak.

But he's never made a radio broadcast, Umeko thought skeptically. We wouldn't know his voice even if we were to hear it.

The next morning the girls gathered in the big assembly hall at Keisen and looked anxiously at the radio placed on the table in the center of the stage. Soon it was turned on, and the voice they heard was indeed that of the Emperor of Japan. "In order to spare the lives of my people," he said in a tense high voice, "I have ordered all hostilities to cease."

Umeko couldn't even remember what he said after that. When the broadcast was over, the girls sat silent and stunned. Then gradually a murmur of voices filled the hall as each of them realized what the broadcast meant. Some of the girls wept softly. "Our country has lost the war," they said sadly. "We have been defeated. It is all over."

For several days, a strange silence fell over Tokyo. Everyone was too shocked to speak or move. The skies were no longer filled with smoke, and the sirens were silent at last. No one seemed to know quite what to do, and they all stumbled through each day as though in a fog. Some of the militarists committed suicide before the Emperor's palace. There were rumors that the American soldiers would soon be in Japan, and fanatics urged that every man, woman, and child should fight them to the bitter end, with bamboo spears if necessary. Police warned women and children to keep off the streets when the Americans arrived, and some even urged that they flee to the hills.

One afternoon Kazu ran over to see Umeko. "I'm being sent away to my aunt's house in Tochigi Prefecture," she told Umeko and her mother in an excited voice. "Father says it won't be safe for women when the American soldiers arrive. Don't you want to come with me?"

Umeko's mother smiled as she listened. "I don't think that will be necessary," she replied. "But, of course, you must do as your father thinks best, and perhaps you will be back by the time school starts again in the fall."

"School!" Kazu said in amazement. "I haven't even thought about going to school again. Father says we'll be lucky just to be alive after the soldiers arrive."

The day after Kazu left, the radio was again full of news, but it was no longer about the Americans. It warned of a giant typhoon that was blowing up from Okinawa and heading straight for Tokyo.

"It isn't enough that the Americans are coming," Umeko complained as she helped Mother and Hana nail boards across the windows, "even the heavens are going to punish us!" She looked at her little vegetable patch and wished there was some way she might save the little potato plants, but there was really nothing she could do. Like the farmers, she would simply have to watch as the fruit of her labors was blown into the sky.

The day the typhoon was to strike, the radio repeatedly issued ominous warnings. Fasten down loose tiles, remove old bath chimneys, have candles ready in case the wires go down, have fresh water ready in case the water supply is cut off. Umeko thought waiting for the typhoon was almost worse than having the great bulk of moving wind and rain come right up to batter the house.

As the sky darkened and the wind shrieked, Umeko crept upstairs to look out through the cracks between the boards at the window. Some of the frail trees in the yard were bent so low, they snapped in two. The garden was swiftly reduced to a shambles, and her potato plants seemed to be torn from the roots and flung into the sky.

The papers called the storm one of the most violent typhoons ever to hit Tokyo, and when it had blown away, it was as though the enemy had struck again. Roofs had blown off, hundreds of frail shacks on the outskirts of the city had been destroyed, hundreds of people had been injured, and, worst of all, the crops had been ruined. Rice that would soon have been ready for harvesting was uprooted, carefully tended vegetable patches had been torn up, and trees had been toppled. Once again, the people of Japan seemed crushed and beaten.

Then, on the twenty-eighth day of the eighth month, 1945, the Americans arrived. Umeko listened closely as the radio reported hundreds of ships steaming into Tokyo Bay, carrying American soldiers in full combat gear. Over them hovered an air umbrella of thousands of planes, and at Atsugi Airport General MacArthur himself came down from the skies in a silver plane to begin the official occupation of Japan.

Umeko wrote long letters to Kazu, telling her of all that was happening in Tokyo. "The radio commentator tells us to have courage," she wrote. "He says that by tomorrow the American troops will be marching through the streets of Tokyo. I wonder what is going to happen to us?"

CHAPTER SEVEN

HE AMERICAN SOLDIERS CAME TO JAPAN, FILTERING
gradually into the streets of Tokyo, sometimes riding out
toward Umeko's house in noisy jeeps that sent everyone running for cover. But they were not the barbarians everyone
thought they would be. They smiled and shouted, "Hello,"
and gave candy and gum to children who had forgotten the
taste of sugar. They rode streetcars and insisted on giving their
seats to women, making the Japanese men do the same.

"They're really very nice," Umeko wrote to Kazu. "I wish
you could come back to Tokyo and see for yourself. I'll go talk
to your father one of these days and see if I can convince him."

Not so long afterward, Umeko found just the opportunity
she needed to see Kazu's parents. One day an American mis-
sionary who had received a food package from the United
States sent some butter and bacon to the Kagawas.

"We simply can't indulge in all this luxury alone," Umeko's mother had said immediately. "Why don't you take a little over to Kazu's mother?"

And so Umeko had her chance. Carrying the tiny parcel, more precious now than gold itself, she walked down the road she had traveled so often to school. Now, instead of neat uniformed classmates, however, she met bedraggled people trudging wearily toward small shacks along the side of the road, dirty and tired and filled with despair. They had no homes, no fuel for bathing, no soap for washing, no medicine for the sick. Umeko couldn't bear to look at them, thinking especially how hungry they must be. She clutched her parcel close to her chest and hurried to Kazu's house, keeping her eyes fixed straight on the road ahead.

As she approached the house, she could see a small cluster of people standing in front, and in the center of everything was an American soldier and his jeep. The soldier was pointing down the road and talking earnestly to Kazu's father. Umeko swallowed hard. Maybe Mr. Takahashi's in trouble, she thought. Now, he'll never let Kazu come home.

She made her way toward the group and heard the soldier saying, "If you could just tell me which road to take to get back to To-ki-o." He pointed down the road. "Do I make a left turn at the next fork?" He was red and perspiring, but Mr. Takahashi stood silent, his hands folded across his chest, glaring grimly at the young soldier.

"He's just lost, Mr. Takahashi," Umeko spoke up from the edge of the group. "He wants to know how to get back into town."

Kazu's father looked startled to see Umeko. "What are you doing here, Umeko San?" he asked. "Get inside quickly. I'm not sure what this soldier will do."

"But I understand what he's saying," Umeko insisted. "He's just asking for directions. He's lost."

Now the soldier pulled a package of American cigarettes from his pocket. He handed them to Mr. Takahashi with a slight bow. "For you, *dozo*," he urged. Then, he went to his jeep and returned with a handful of candy bars and gum for the others who watched. They backed away, not quite sure whether they should accept these wonderful gifts, but Umeko was too excited to be shy.

"Chocolate! Real American chocolate!" she shouted, and, gratefully accepting the soldier's gift, she said in her best Keisen English, "Thank you. Thank you very much."

The soldier's face brightened in a happy smile. "Hey, you speak English!" he said. "Listen, tell this gentleman I'm not here to steal his land or do him any harm. I just want him to show me which of these roads will take me back to To-ki-o. I've been going around in circles for the last hour!"

Umeko nodded and explained once again to Mr. Takahashi. He still eyed the soldier with suspicion, but now he bent down and with a stick drew in the dirt a map of the roads nearby. He traced his stick lightly over the route that would take the soldier back to Tokyo, and when he had finished, the soldier gave him a grateful pat on the back.

"Thanks a lot, mister," he said. "I get it now." And then, standing straight and tall, he bowed from the waist. "*Arigato!*" he called. He jumped into his jeep, waved good-by to the onlookers, and was off with a roar.

They all watched as the jeep disappeared down the road in a cloud of dust. One of the women shook her head in astonishment. "He seemed like such a nice young man," she said, as though genuinely surprised that he had not pulled out a gun and shot them all down.

Mr. Takahashi seemed more puzzled than any of them. "I don't understand," he said slowly. "It is very difficult to understand."

"What is?" Umeko ventured.

"Why, he is a conquering soldier, Umeko San," Mr. Takahashi explained. "Don't you see, he had the right to strike me or order me to polish his boots or make me grovel in the dirt before him. And, yet, he treated me as an equal. He gave me cigarettes, and he even bowed to say his thanks." Mr. Takahashi shook his head. "Very strange," he murmured. "It is very strange."

But gradually a slow smile crept across his face, and, as he turned toward Umeko, he spoke more cheerfully than he had in a long time. "*Sah*, Umeko San," he said brightly. "Come on in and have some tea with us."

In a few weeks, Kazu came back from Tochigi, and there was no more talk at the Takahashis about having to hide from the barbaric Americans.

Umeko's father came home, too, much sooner than he had expected. A message had come to him from Prince Higashikuni, the new postwar Prime Minister. Although her mother didn't show it, Umeko could tell she was excited.

"Just think," she told Umeko. "The Prime Minister has asked your father to serve as special advisor to the Department of Public Welfare. What a wonderful step forward for Christianity in Japan!"

"And what a difference from last year," Umeko said, shaking her head. "The militarists were all ready to shoot Father then, but now he'll be hobnobbing with the Prime Minister himself."

The news was good on all sides. Miss Tanaka called one day to say that her father had also been asked to serve as an advisor to the new government. Even the Suzukis returned from Akagi Village to help reorganize the church kindergarten.

Although Father was back home, sometimes it seemed as if he were still in hiding, for Umeko was seldom able to see him. Occasionally, she would find him in his study talking with Mr. Suzuki or some other visitor, working out a solution for some new problem of rehabilitation. Sometimes she would stop for a few moments and listen to their conversation.

"It is gratifying to know that the imprisoned Christians have been freed," she heard him say one day. "Now, the next immediate problem is to secure more food and clothing for the refugees. We must act quickly. We must go straight to the top."

A few days later Umeko found her father looking enormously pleased at dinnertime. "This has been a good day, indeed," he said with satisfaction. "General MacArthur agreed to release special rations for our refugees. When I told him we couldn't wait another day, he acted immediately."

"Did you talk to him yourself, Father? Did you really see him?" Umeko asked.

Father nodded. "I did, and he was very gracious." Then, almost in the same breath, he was talking about organizing a pawn shop. "With everyone selling their possessions to get cash for food, we must provide them with a place where they can be sure of a fair price," he said gravely.

"But, Father, what is General MacArthur like?" Umeko persisted. "Is he really so tall? Did you talk to him in English? Was he polite?" She was consumed with curiosity about this American general who commanded the Occupation Troops.

Dr. Kagawa paused. "Yes, yes . . . he was very polite. We talked only briefly," he began, but at that moment the telephone rang, and he rose quickly from the table. "I'll answer it,

Hana San," he said. "That's probably the call I'm expecting. If all goes well, we may be able to get the Consumers' Cooperative started again." And with that he was gone, his dinner half-eaten and Umeko's questions left dangling in mid-air.

Umeko sighed. "He might as well be in Akagi Village for all I hear from him," she murmured.

As the days went on, Umeko noticed that "freedom" and "democracy" and "equality" were words that appeared in almost every publication she read.

"You know what this means?" she asked Kazu one day. "If we're a democracy now, it means we're free to think and act just as we please. We don't have to obey the Emperor or his officials or the police or anybody!"

Kazu nodded slowly. "I know, that's what everyone says, but somehow I just can't stop doing the things I've been taught to do all my life. Can you?"

Umeko thought for a moment. She had always longed to be free from authority and restrictions. She had always longed to do exactly as she pleased. "I don't know," she said. "I think maybe this is our big chance."

"Our chance?" Kazu asked. "What do you mean?"

"I mean for all of us—especially girls and women of Japan," Umeko explained. "It's our chance to become really free, as individuals."

"Why, you make yourself sound grown up," Kazu said laughing. "You must have been talking with Tanaka San again."

But Umeko shook her head. "After all, I am sixteen now, and I've been thinking about lots of things."

"But this democracy," Kazu continued, shaking her head, "I don't think I really understand it at all."

Umeko spoke boldly to Kazu, but down deep she, too, felt

a strange tug of war inside. It was difficult to explain. Suddenly, everything she had ever learned seemed to be wrong. It was like taking years and years to fit the pieces of a puzzle together carefully and then, suddenly, being told that the pieces should really be flung into the air.

Schools opened again in the fall, but most of the texts they had used before were now banned. No more Japanese history was to be taught until new, approved books could be written. The whole Japanese school system was revised, and every teacher seemed to be feeling his way cautiously amid vast confusion.

"We'll never be ready for college entrance exams in March at this rate," Kazu said mournfully.

But Umeko consoled her with a hopeful thought. "Well, at least everyone else will be just as confused and ignorant as we are."

As the months passed, the new ways gradually seemed the right ways to Umeko and Kazu and their friends. Everything from the West seemed alive and fresh; everything Japanese seemed old and wrong.

Umeko stopped taking the tea ceremony lessons she had continued since she was a child. "It's a new world now," she told her mother. "The tea ceremony is really old fashioned."

Miss Tanaka agreed that life in Japan was changing. "Yes, the vertical society seems to be disappearing at last," she said.

"I'm not sure I know what you mean," Umeko confessed.

"I mean society built like a ladder—with everyone on a proper rung, obeying orders from the top down," she explained. "Now we can think horizontally, beginning with the individual and working out toward the family and the community and society from there. Now perhaps women can have more freedom to live as individual personalities."

83

"With a chance to express ourselves," Umeko added.

"Exactly," Miss Tanaka agreed. She had often talked to Umeko about the role of women in Japan, and lately Umeko felt the full impact of all that she told her. She remembered now what Mrs. Suzuki had said about the women in Akagi Village. "They must be treated as something more than housekeepers and cooks," she had said indignantly.

Mother was pleased when Umeko showed interest in the new horizons for Japanese women. "Perhaps some day you'll do some of the work I've wanted to do for our women," she said. "It's a problem that's been in my heart a long, long time."

Umeko felt again the fleeting desire to serve others as her mother and Mrs. Suzuki had done, but the glitter of her own daydreams persisted, and, as always, they won out rather quickly over her loftier aims.

By the time New Year's was at hand, the pieces of the puzzle were flung farther than Umeko dreamed they ever could be. The Emperor, whom the Japanese people had worshiped as a descendant of the sun goddess, issued a proclamation that he was not divine, that he was an ordinary human being just like his people. From the rubble and ruin of war, a new world truly seemed to be emerging in Japan. A new constitution abolishing war was to be created; for the first time in their lives Japanese women would be voting in the postwar elections; there would be equality of education for all; and freedom of thought, speech, and assembly would prevail. The factories that had been producing guns would now make machinery for peace.

"Japan is going to be a new and wonderful country," Umeko declared happily to Hana.

"Oh, I agree with you," Hana said solemnly. "And I intend to make this the best New Year's we've ever had."

"But there's nothing to eat," Umeko reminded her wistfully.

"How will you ever make a New Year's feast without food?"

Hana grinned. "Oh, I've saved a few things," she said slyly, "and I've taken a few trips out to the country to shop. After all, your brother and sister are coming home from medical school and your father said he would be back from his trip to Shinkawa in time for New Year's. We must welcome them home with something."

"Just think," Umeko murmured, "we'll all be home together this New Year's. Everyone'll be here, except Toshio."

Hana sighed softly. "He was such a nice boy."

"Hana San, do you think he's dead?" Umeko asked thoughtfully.

Hana shook her head. "It's hard to say, Umeko Chan. I just don't know."

"But we would have heard if he had died," Umeko reasoned. "I just feel sure he's safe and alive somewhere."

"Well, I hope you're right," Hana conceded, but even as she spoke she shook her head in doubt.

It was like old times on New Year's Day even though there was scarcely any food for the celebration. Umeko's brother and sister had come home the night before, and the house seemed to burst with laughter and talk. On New Year's morning, the Suzukis were the first to arrive to wish everyone a good new year. "How wonderful it is to be together again," they said gratefully, "and to know that the war is at an end."

Umeko's father nodded and said, "I pray that from it all Japan can come closer to becoming a Christian and peace-loving nation."

As the talk grew serious, Umeko slipped outside to watch for Kazu. She had promised to come over as soon as she could get away from her family's celebration. The sun was bright, and the day felt clean and fresh, just as the first day of a new year

85

should. Umeko looked up, feeling the warmth of the sun on her face and scanning the sky for any bright new kites.

"What are you doing, still watching for planes?" a voice called to her. It was Kazu, who ran quickly to her side and whispered furtively. "Let's hurry inside. A dirty, miserable-looking soldier's been following me all the way down the road. I don't dare look back, but I think he's still close behind."

Umeko looked up. "It's too late," she said. "There he is, coming through the gate."

The soldier was thin and unshaven, and the rims of his eyes were strangely red against the paleness of his cheeks. His uniform was rumpled and worn as though he had spent many a night and day in it. He walked slowly toward Umeko and Kazu.

"He's probably sick and come to beg for food," Umeko said. "Come on, let's go inside."

But as they turned to go in, the soldier called out, "Umeko San, don't you know me?" As Umeko turned and stared at the soldier, she covered her mouth to stop the scream that almost slipped out. Could this poor worn-out soldier be Toshio? Umeko felt as though she was seeing a ghost.

"Toshio San!" she cried at last. "Is it really you?"

The soldier nodded. "More dead than alive, I'm afraid, but still me. You've both grown," he added, in an effort to make conversation. But Umeko no longer listened. She ran inside shouting at the top of her voice, "It's Toshio San. He's come home. Mother! Father! Everybody, come see!"

Soon, everyone had run to the veranda at the side of the house, and they all greeted Toshio.

"*Mah, mah,* Toshio San," Mrs. Kagawa exclaimed, taking both his hands in hers. "How grateful I am to have all my children home at last."

When the excitement died down a bit and Toshio was sit-

86

ting with them at the big table to have some tea, he looked around as though he were seeing each of them for the first time.

"I thought I would never see you again," he said quietly. "It is like a dream."

"But tell us where you've been," Umeko begged. "Why didn't you write? Didn't you get any of my letters?"

Toshio looked down at the table and spoke in a voice so low it was hard to hear what he said.

"I was in the Philippines when the Americans came," he began. "My two friends were killed, but I was not so fortunate. I was taken prisoner."

So that was why he has been silent, Umeko thought.

Toshio went on, almost as though he were forcing himself to speak. "I neither fought nor died for my country," he said bitterly. "I'm a disgrace—a failure. I had no right to return to a country I couldn't serve."

Umeko's father put a hand on his arm to stop him. "Toshio San, you must never think that," he said firmly. "There is much you can do now to help rebuild our country. We are grateful that you were spared and that you returned healthy and well."

"My relatives in Hokkaido didn't feel that way at all," Toshio answered.

"In Hokkaido?" Umeko was surprised. "Did you go back to your uncle's place, then?"

Toshio nodded. "My transport docked there, and I had nowhere else to go. I thought maybe he'd let me stay until I could decide what to do with myself."

"But he didn't? What did he say?" Umeko questioned. "Why didn't you come back to Tokyo right away?"

Umeko's sister nudged her. "Goodness, Umeko," she whispered. "Give him a chance to talk."

Everyone leaned forward to listen as Toshio went on.

"There were three families living in my uncle's house—all refugees from Tokyo," he explained. "They had no spare quilts for me, and there was barely enough food to go around. I knew my uncle was ashamed of me. He asked me not to tell anyone I had been a prisoner. I knew he wanted me to leave. I stayed only two days and decided to come back to Tokyo."

"And we're certainly glad you did," Dr. Kagawa said warmly. "It's a real blessing to have you back."

"Yes, you're home now," Mrs. Kagawa added quickly. "This is where you belong."

"You're all very kind," Toshio said briefly. "Thank you for welcoming a failure of a soldier!"

Umeko found herself staring at Toshio. Something was wrong. Umeko knew he was pale and thin and tired. His face had grown angular and his eyes were sunken, but it was more than that. Something inside seemed to have shriveled up and died since she last saw him. She remembered how they had laughed and joked and had such good times together.

"That's what's wrong with him," Umeko said to Kazu later that day. "Toshio doesn't laugh any more. In fact, I think he's even forgotten how to smile."

"But think of all he's been through," Kazu answered. "You've got to give him time."

"I know," Umeko agreed. "I know he needs time, but somehow he makes me feel uncomfortable. I wish he'd relax and just be his old self."

"He will," Kazu said softly. "I'm sure he will."

But Umeko was to discover that it wasn't going to be such a simple matter.

CHAPTER EIGHT

A WEEK WENT BY. THEN TWO AND THREE, AND STILL TOSHIO seemed wrapped up in his strange, moody silence. He was out much of the time, and when he was home he stayed in his room with the door closed. Even when he ate with the family, he had little to say, and Umeko noticed that he kept his eyes on his plate much of the time.

"We must make him feel wanted and useful," Umeko's mother said one day. "Now that he's had time to get rested, I think we must try to get him to participate a little more in activities around the house."

Umeko had what she thought was a brilliant idea. "Do you suppose he'd help me with my geometry?" she asked. "I've just got to brush up on it if I'm ever going to pass the college entrance exams in March."

"He might," Mother answered. "Why don't you ask him?"

The very next day, as soon as Umeko came home from school, she went up to Toshio's room and knocked on the door. There was a moment's silence and then a crisp military, "*Hai?*" Umeko was delighted to find him home.

"Will you come down and have three o'clock tea with me?" she began. "I have something I want to ask you. I need your help."

"All right," Toshio answered. "I'll be down in a minute." He hurried downstairs and soon was sitting down across the table from Umeko.

She thrust a dish of steamed sweet potatoes toward him saying, "Have a potato—for a change!"

Toshio smiled. "Seems to me you've been eating sweet potatoes ever since I've known you," he said. "You used to keep the little Potato Lady in business, didn't you?"

Umeko nodded. "I did until she couldn't get any more oil and had to close up her shop."

Toshio took a gulp of hot tea. "Well," he began, "what's on your mind? Still getting into trouble doing things you shouldn't?"

Umeko grinned. Toshio was actually beginning to sound like his old self. "Oh, I do that all the time," Umeko admitted, "but that's not why I need your help. I'm getting ready for college entrance exams in March, and I was wondering if you'd help me with my geometry."

"College entrance exams," Toshio murmured. "So you're entering college!"

"Well, I hope I am," Umeko added. "Kazu and I both want to go to Tsuda College."

Toshio nodded, but he no longer seemed to be listening. "College exams . . . ," he said almost to himself. And Umeko remembered then that he had not been able to finish college.

"Toshio San, you ought to go back to school, too," she said eagerly. "It would be nice for you to get your degree."

Toshio looked at Umeko, and then suddenly he laughed a hard, humorless laugh. "A degree?" he said mockingly. "What good is a degree today? Just look at Japan," he said, talking on as though all the thoughts he'd harbored alone were suddenly spilling out at once. "All our cities burned to rubble; millions of people roaming the streets starving and homeless and without work; millions more coming back from the colonies we lost to clutter up our small miserable islands. And why? Because we fought a useless, stupid, impossible war. Because we listened to leaders who lied and deceived us."

Toshio's eyes glittered and his cheeks were flushed. "We're beaten and ruined, Umeko San. Where's our great East Asia Co-Prosperity Sphere now? What hope is there for Japan now? The truth is, there is no hope. No hope at all!"

"But you can't say there's no hope at all," Umeko burst in. "At least we're free now. We can learn about democracy. Women will be able to vote and there'll be equality of education and there's the new constitution . . . . " Umeko grasped at every constructive thought that occured to her. She just couldn't sit there and let Toshio talk that way.

"Freedom!" Toshio said bitterly. "Freedom to work and starve ourselves to death. Very nice! And what's the use of a new constitution? There'll be war again as long as we let capitalists run Japan. They'll keep the farmers and laborers wallowing in debt, keep the spoils, and plunge us into another stupid war."

"But the militarists got us into this war," Umeko began, not able to sort out the jumbled thoughts of Toshio's outburst. He was simply flinging a string of complaints at her as fast as he could think of them, and they didn't make sense. Umeko knew if she just had time to think, she could show him he was wrong.

In her frustration, she said simply, "Toshio San, you sound just like a Communist!"

Toshio looked startled. He took a deep breath and murmured sheepishly, "I'm sorry. I was carried away. I'm afraid I talked too much."

Umeko kept her eyes on him. "Well, are you?" she asked.

"Am I what?"

"A Communist?"

Toshio started to say something and then thought better of it. "About the geometry," he said abruptly, "I'd like to help you, but you know I never finished college. And, besides, I think I left my brains back in the Philippines. I'm no good any more, Umeko San. You'd better get someone else to help you."

"But you always used to help me before," Umeko persisted. "You knew so much about everything."

It was no use. Toshio stood up and edged toward the door. "I'm sorry," he murmured, "but you understand, don't you?"

Umeko nodded, but she really didn't understand at all. For just a few moments, she thought she had found the old Toshio once more, but how wrong she'd been. She knew now that he was more mixed up and unhappy than she'd imagined.

She tried to tell her mother all that he had said. She wanted somehow to convey his bitter cynicism, but as she tried to repeat his tirade, she gave up saying, "Oh, he's just impossible." Soon her mind was so full of preparing for her exams, she simply didn't have any more time to worry about Toshio.

Mr. Suzuki offered to coach her in geometry saying, "I know exactly how you feel. Why, I still have nightmares about my own examinations, and I took them over twenty years ago!"

"Do you really?" Umeko sighed. "I've been having the most horrible dreams about mine, and I seem to fail every time."

"I know," Mr. Suzuki sympathized, "that's how my nightmares always ended, too. But cheer up," he added, "when I finally did take the exams, I passed without any trouble at all."

Umeko studied harder than she had ever studied before, often reading by the flickering light of a candle while the current was turned off all over the city to conserve electricity.

"I'll be so glad when this is all over," Kazu would say as they compared notes on their struggle to conquer the impossible amount of knowledge that lay before them. "Sometimes I wonder if it's worth all the trouble."

"Well, you want to be a teacher, don't you?" Umeko asked.

Kazu nodded. "And you've got to become a great writer some day," she said. "I guess we both have a long way to go yet."

"But just think, Kazu, when we finish school, we can really be free and independent," Umeko added, and with this pleasant thought in mind, she plunged even harder into her studies.

March 3 crept up on her so suddenly, Umeko almost forgot about the Doll Festival. Before the war, it was a day she looked forward to for weeks. Umeko remembered the excitement of arranging her precious festival dolls on their red tiers, placing peach blossoms and rice cakes in front of them, and inviting her friends to tea. She remembered how they all came in their best silk kimono, fluttering about like heavy-winged butterflies, chattering and giggling till it was almost time for supper. This always seemed the most wonderful day of the year until May, when her brother had the Boys' Festival all to himself. Then, Umeko would watch him hoist the big cloth carp on the bamboo pole, and, as it fluttered in the brisk breeze, she would long to have a carp of her own flying up there beside his. I should have been a boy, she would think wistfully, then I'd have my own carp swimming up there in the river of the sky.

During the war, of course, no one had had time for festivals, but now that it was over, it didn't seem right to ignore March 3. Umeko opened the trunk in which her dolls had been stored. The little wooden boxes with the dolls wrapped in wads of soft cotton were placed in neat rows, just as Mother had left them.

"I just don't have time to get you all out," Umeko apologized to the dolls as she fingered the dozens of boxes. "If I just didn't have so much to do. . . . " Then she had another of her brilliant ideas. She looked for the box in which the Emperor and Empress dolls were stored and carried it quickly to her room. She placed the dolls carefully on top of her bookcase and put beside them a spray of flowering peach. Two caramels went on the little lacquer dish before them. It was a good thing caramels were being made again now instead of soldiers' biscuits.

Umeko stepped back to look at her display. "There," she said, quite pleased with herself, "you two will have to represent your whole court this year!" She bowed with a flourish and returned to her studies with a clear conscience. She'd been able to take care of the Doll Festival after all.

The entrance examinations at Tsuda College took three full days. Each day as Kazu and Umeko got on the train, they would see other students bending over books, using every minute to cram a little more knowledge into their aching heads. It was time for entrance examinations at all colleges, and everywhere Umeko looked she saw worried students looking pale and anxious.

At Tsuda two-hour written examinations were given each morning and afternoon, and then a final oral examination on the last afternoon. One by one, each girl who applied for entrance was interviewed and questioned by a group of professors.

"I thought I would die of fright," Kazu admitted when it was all over. She held out her hands to show Umeko. "Look," she said sheepishly, "I've bitten all my nails down to little stubs!"

"I don't even know what I was doing with my hands," Umeko admitted. "I was probably doing something stupid like scratching my nose! Now, how are we ever going to wait until they post results?"

"I don't know," Kazu murmured. "It'll seem like years."

"But you know," Umeko said cheerfully, "I have a feeling we both passed."

That night, however, a knot of worry began to grow inside Umeko. Suppose she didn't pass. Or, worse still, suppose one of them passed and the other didn't. After all, there were always so many applicants for college, and everyone knew that only one out of five would be able to enter. That meant lots of girls would be dropped out even if they did well on the tests. Umeko shuddered at the thought, and again she would dream that she had failed and wake up with her heart pounding.

"Thank goodness," she'd murmur as she realized it was only a dream, and she would tell herself again that she and Kazu simply had to be among the lucky ones.

On the morning the results were to be posted, Kazu came to call for Umeko so they could go together to the college.

"Feel my hands," Kazu said as she took Umeko's. "They're like ice."

Umeko shivered. "So are mine."

"Did you have any breakfast?" Kazu asked.

"Only tea," Umeko admitted. "I couldn't eat a thing."

"Neither could I. Not even a bowl of rice."

They sat silently at the entrance of Umeko's house, looking down at their shoes.

"Well," Umeko said at last. "I guess we've got to go some-time. Let's get it over with."

Kazu nodded. "I want to know so badly, and yet I'm scared to death to go see," she admitted. Umeko knew exactly how she felt.

When they got to Tsuda, it wasn't yet nine o'clock but already the halls were crowded with girls who had come early to be among the first to know. No one talked much, and everyone looked grim. At ten minutes to nine o'clock, there was a small flurry of excitement. A clerk had just come from the office with some papers that he proceeded to tack up on the bulletin board, and now with a sudden rush, the girls pushed and shoved their way toward him.

"Just a moment," he shouted. "Please, wait a moment, young ladies."

But no one listened to him. He was barely able to tack up all the sheets before he was engulfed. The names were listed alphabetically, and Kazu edged her way toward the K's, saying to Umeko, "Let's look at yours first." And there, at the very head of the list of K's was Umeko's name: KAGAWA, UMEKO—PASSED.

"Oh, Umeko! I knew it!" Kazu shouted. They hugged each other and shrieked with joy. Everywhere around them other girls were screaming and shouting as they discovered they had passed. But nearby there were also others who stood silently, trying to fight back the tears.

"Now yours," Umeko urged. "Come on, hurry!" They pushed their way toward the T's. There were always dozens of Takahashis on any list, and Umeko put a finger on the sheet and ran down the long list of Takahashis.

TAKAHASHI, AYAKO . . . TAKAHASHI, CHIYO . . . TAKAHASHI, FUKIKO . . . and at last, TAKAHASHI, KAZU—FAILED.

"But that can't be right!" Umeko cried. "That must be wrong!"

96

"No, it isn't. I've failed, Umeko, I've failed," Kazu said, and suddenly she buried her face in her hands and began to sob. "I won't be able to go to college with you. We can't study together any more. I'll never be a teacher!"

Umeko searched for words to comfort Kazu. "We'll check at the office," she said. "Maybe they made a mistake. Maybe they put the wrong mark up after your name. They do make mistakes, you know."

She pulled Kazu along to the office, but the door was closed and a sign posted reading, "All inquiries regarding examination results must be made in writing."

Umeko felt as though a bucket of ice water had been poured over her. She had been so happy a moment ago, and now life seemed all wrong. How could she go on to college without Kazu? They'd always done everything together until now.

"We'll think of something," she said to Kazu. "We've got to."

But Kazu was red eyed and silent. She walked to the station without uttering a word, and they rode home in gloomy silence. At Shinjuku Station they got off to change trains. "Be careful," Umeko called back to Kazu as she stepped off onto the crowded platform. She moved out beyond the crowds that waited to push into their train and then turned to say something to Kazu. But Kazu was nowhere in sight.

"Kazu!" Umeko shouted, as she glanced about the crowds. "Kazu Chan!"

She made her way down the length of the platform, pushing and shoving as she moved among the milling people. With trains pulling in and out at two minute intervals, this was the most congested station in all of Tokyo.

"Of all places to disappear," Umeko muttered frantically. "How will I ever find her?" She tried to think what she might do if she were in Kazu's place. Would she roam the streets of Shinjuku? Would she go somewhere to see a friend? But Umeko knew Kazu would talk to no one if she wouldn't talk to her. Maybe she just wanted to go on home alone, Umeko thought at last and decided she'd better hurry home and tell Mother what had happened.

"Mother!" she called frantically as she ran into the house.

Her mother took one look at her and asked, "Did you fail, Ume Chan?"

Umeko shook her head. "No, I passed, but it's Kazu. She failed, and now she's disappeared somewhere and I can't find her. What am I going to do?" Umeko was close to tears as she told her mother what had happened at Shinjuku Station. "Do you suppose she's gone on home?" Umeko asked hopefully.

Mrs. Kagawa looked troubled. She thought of the hundreds of students who fail their college entrance examinations each year and of those who were despondent enough to take their own lives. Usually, they were boys who knew that without a college degree they could never find a good job, boys who knew that a college education might make the difference between a life of success or failure. Surely Kazu Chan would not feel that desperate, thought Mrs. Kagawa. Surely she would do nothing foolish, and, yet, she has always been such a sensitive child.

"Ume Chan," she said, "you must go tell Kazu's mother what happened. I wish I could go with you, but I must meet with the Women's Guild this afternoon. Try to tell Takahashi San gently."

Umeko nodded and hurried toward Kazu's house, but all the way her heart pounded as she wondered how she could face Kazu's mother. What would she say? How could she tell her? If only Kazu would be there when she arrived!

Umeko looked out beyond the road at the mountains that

seemed to rise dimly from a gray mist. From somewhere the delicate scent of peach blossoms seemed to drift to her in the warm spring air, but even this brought no comfort. Umeko felt as though a great weight had suddenly flung itself around her shoulders and refused to let go.

Umeko reached Kazu's house and slid the front door open gently. Kazu's mother hurried to the door. "Kazu Chan?" she called and then, "Ah, it's you, Umeko Chan."

Umeko looked at Kazu's mother, searching for a way to tell her what had happened, but words weren't necessary.

"Kazu has failed?" Mrs. Takahashi asked as soon as she saw Umeko.

Umeko nodded. "And . . . and . . . she left me at Shinjuku. I don't know where she is. I . . . I hoped she'd be home. I feel so awful," and suddenly Umeko began to cry. "Kazu Chan knew just as much as I did. It just wasn't right for her to fail. It wasn't fair," she sobbed.

Mrs. Takahashi sighed softly. "There are always those who must fail," she said. "Kazu Chan is one of the unlucky ones. The gods never smiled too kindly on that child," she added. "But never mind, Ume Chan. Don't feel so bad. Come in and wait with me. I think she will be home soon." It was Mrs. Takahashi who comforted Umeko.

But as they waited together, Kazu's mother glanced at the clock every few minutes. Her lips trembled, and she grew pale. "Where could she have gone?" she murmured. "If she isn't back soon, I must call her father from the fields."

Umeko knew how annoyed Mr. Takahashi would be to learn that Kazu had not only failed but had also run off somewhere. "Hurry home, Kazu Chan," she murmured. "Hurry home before your father has to be called."

"If she does not come in another hour," Mrs. Takahashi

said slowly, "perhaps we must ask the police to help us. I can think of no one she could have gone to. She didn't have enough money to go to her aunt's in Tochigi or anywhere else outside of Tokyo." Mrs. Takahashi wrung her hands until the knuckles showed white. "Kazu Chan, please come home," she begged.

"If only I could think where she might have gone," Umeko said again and again.

But suddenly Mrs. Takahashi looked up. "Listen," she said. It was the sound of a car on the road, coming closer and closer, and finally stopping in front of the house.

"That must be Kazu!" Umeko cried.

Kazu's mother rushed to the door and ran outside. "Kazu Chan! Kazu Chan!" she cried, taking her in her arms. "Where in the world have you been?" But Kazu was sobbing and couldn't talk.

"Oh, Kazu Chan, we were so worried about you," Umeko said. And then, she noticed the American soldier and his jeep. The soldier stood awkwardly with his cap in his hand, smiling just a little as he watched Kazu and her mother.

"I found her wandering around Shibuya," the soldier explained. "She was in such a daze I almost ran into her with my jeep. I thought she was sick and tried to get her to a hospital, but she insisted on coming home. Boy, I never thought 'home' would be so hard to find," he said with a grin. "Seems as if we've wandered around these roads for hours."

"But how wonderful that you brought her back," Umeko said. "We were so afraid something terrible had happened to her."

Mrs. Takahashi turned now and bowed to the soldier. "Domo arigato gozai mashita," she said, thanking him, but she did not invite him to come in.

The soldier grinned good-naturedly and bowed back. He

stood for a moment, not quite knowing what to do; but now Kazu bowed to him, too. "Thank you," she said softly. "You have been most kind."

"It was a pleasure," the soldier answered with a smile. "And now that you're home safely, I guess I'll be on my way."

He turned to go, but before he left, he paused a moment. He put a hand gently on Kazu's shoulder, and Umeko heard him say softly, "I'll be seeing you."

T HE NEXT MORNING KAZU CAME TO SEE UMEKO IMMEDI-
ately after breakfast. She still looked pale, and there were
dark circles beneath her eyes.

"I've got to talk with you," she whispered to Umeko. "Will
you come for a walk with me?"

"Sure," Umeko agreed, wondering why Kazu asked her to
go out of the house in order to talk.

"Are you all right?" Umeko asked anxiously as they hurried
outside. They walked down the road toward the open fields.

"I guess I was silly to run off like that yesterday," Kazu said.
"But I felt so terrible, I just wanted to die. I hoped a car or
train would run over me."

"Oh, Kazu, it isn't that bad," Umeko said quickly. "You can
always try again next year. In the meantime, you can go to
one of those special schools that coach you for the exams."

Kazu shook her head. "I couldn't bear to go through all this again," she said. "And anyway," she added slowly, "I don't care any more. I never was very good at studies, and I don't think I'd make a good teacher after all."

"Kazu, don't talk like that," Umeko scolded. "That's just silly." But Kazu was looking off to the distance now, and Umeko could see that she was not paying any attention to what she was saying.

The two girls walked on silently, past the rows of houses and the children who clattered about them in their wooden *geta*. Soon the girls came to the edge of the woods, and Umeko stopped for a moment. "Listen," she said softly, "that's a nightingale."

Kazu stood still and held her breath. The suggestion of a smile curved at her lips. "Spring is really here, isn't it?" she whispered.

As they walked on through the shadowy forest, Kazu turned to Umeko. "Do you remember Tom San, the soldier who brought me home yesterday?" she asked.

Umeko could almost see the sandy-haired American with the blue eyes and the quick grin. "Of course," she said. "He was nice, wasn't he?"

"Yes," Kazu agreed quickly, "and he was so very kind to me. You know, I stepped right in front of his jeep. It was my fault that he nearly hit me, but he insisted on bringing me home. He said I didn't look at all well. I suppose it was from all that crying."

"You did look pretty awful when you got home," Umeko agreed.

"Well, I promised to meet him in town today," Kazu blurted out.

"You're meeting the soldier?" Umeko asked. "Alone?"

Kazu nodded. "He said he needed someone to help him with some shopping, and, besides, I thought I should thank him properly for his kindness to me yesterday. Oh, Umeko," Kazu asked anxiously, "do you think it's wrong? Do you think I shouldn't go?"

Umeko thought of some of the stories she had heard about American soldiers. "Well," she said doubtfully, "I just don't know. He did seem nice, though."

"What would you do if you were in my place?" Kazu asked at last.

Umeko thought only a moment, and then she knew. "Why, I guess I'd go," she said with a grin. "Besides, there can't be any harm in meeting him just once. He was awfully good to you."

Kazu smiled. "I thought that's what you'd say. I needed somebody to help me make up my mind. I didn't dare tell my mother about it," she admitted. "I'll tell her I'm going to town with you, Umeko Chan. Be careful not to say anything."

"I promise," Umeko said, "if you'll promise to come over first thing tomorrow and tell me all about what you do today."

Kazu held out her little finger and locked it with Umeko's. "Gemma, I promise," she said, and she started down the road. "See you tomorrow, then," she called back, and already the sadness of the day before seemed to have flickered away.

All the rest of the day, Umeko thought about Kazu and the soldier. She wondered where they would go and what they would do. She wondered if Kazu would be able to understand him. Umeko thought she would burst with the keeping of such a big secret that threatened to explode into the open so many times that day.

Kazu kept her promise and came early the next day to tell Umeko what had happened. "Oh, Umeko, it was so much fun," Kazu confided. "Tom San took me to see a real American movie."

"An American movie!" Umeko shrieked. "Where?"

"In a special theatre in Hibiya," Kazu explained. "It's just for American soldiers and their guests. And, Umeko, we ate chocolate bars and popcorn and had Coca Cola that came out of a big red machine!"

Umeko had never seen Kazu so excited before. Her cheeks were flushed, her eyes sparkled, and she even forgot about keeping her voice down.

Umeko put a finger to her lips. "Not too loud," she whispered. And then she went on with a sigh, "Just think, Kazu, you've been on a real date. Just like the girls in America!"

"And with an American soldier, too," Kazu added. "It still seems like a dream."

"I just hope your father never finds out," Umeko said. "Wouldn't he be scandalized?"

Kazu shuddered at the thought. "He'd probably say I've soiled the Takahashi name forever. I've got to be awfully careful he doesn't find out about Tom San."

"Well, don't worry about me," Umeko said quickly. "I'll never tell. I'll guard your secret!"

Kazu leaned closer to Umeko. "Can you keep another one?" she whispered.

"Another secret? What is it?"

"Well . . . ," Kazu began shyly. "I promised to meet him again next Saturday."

This time Umeko couldn't keep her own voice down. "Did you really?" she asked incredulously.

Kazu nodded. "I did. I promised before I quite realized what I was doing," she admitted lamely. "You see, we didn't have time for any of that shopping yesterday, and when he asked if I'd help him with it next week, I just said 'yes.' After all, that's the least I can do for him, don't you think?" Kazu asked.

"You're really turning into a modern girl, aren't you?" Umeko said, laughing.

"Do you think I shouldn't go?" Kazu asked anxiously. "Is it wrong?"

Umeko shook her head. "Why should it be wrong?" she said. "After all, we're free now to do as we please, and what harm could there be in meeting him just once more?"

"None at all, I guess," Kazu answered.

So once more she went to meet the American soldier on Saturday. It wasn't the last time, however, for Kazu found herself promising to meet him just once more, and then just once again after that. And soon she was meeting him regularly every Saturday afternoon.

Umeko noticed that Kazu gradually emerged from the shell of shyness into which she so often shrank back, and she talked more and more of such things as freedom and equality for women.

"If we're free to do as we please," she said one day to Umeko, "then we're free to marry anyone we please, aren't we?"

"Of course," Umeko began, and then quickly she asked, "Why? Do you have someone special in mind?"

Kazu shook her head vigorously. "Oh, no! No, I don't," she said. "It's just that I was thinking how nice it would be to choose the man I want to marry myself, instead of having Mother and Father pick him out for me."

"That's how it should be," Umeko agreed, but she looked closely at Kazu, wondering if she had something she was trying to say. Kazu kept her secret thoughts carefully guarded, however, and the bright smile she turned toward Umeko revealed nothing more.

Before long, it was time for the cherry trees to blossom again, and the bare dark branches of the willow were covered with the frothy green of budding leaves. If it hadn't been for the war, everyone would be getting out their spring kimono and planning flower-viewing parties, Umeko thought. It would be a time for festivals and bamboo-shoot digging and all sorts of happy activities. But since the war, no one had time to think of anything but finding enough food to keep alive, and even spring seemed overshadowed by the drabness of a country that still struggled to dig itself out of the misery of war.

For Umeko, however, this spring did have many special meanings, for there was graduation from Keisen and the beginning of a new life at Tsuda College. It seemed strange not to have Kazu come along, and as Umeko went to her new classes she felt lonely and lost. There were a few other girls from Keisen, but it wasn't like having Kazu. Life at college was bewildering and strange, and, once again, Umeko thought of asking for Toshio's help. But these days Toshio was scarcely ever at home.

"What in the world is Toshio San doing these days?" Umeko asked one day. And then almost as if in answer to her question, the police arrived again to talk to Father.

"What is it this time?" Umeko asked her mother. "What's Father done now?"

"I'm afraid it isn't Father," her mother said sadly. "Toshio San hasn't been home for two days."

Umeko remembered how often Toshio stayed away these days and how he had asked Mother not to worry when he didn't come home. "I'm with friends," he said simply, and that was all. She remembered how she'd often been awakened in the darkness of night by his footsteps as he crept softly to his room. What in the world had he done to bring the police?

As soon as the police left, Umeko and her mother hurried to Father's study.

"What is it?" Mother asked. "Is it Toshio San?"

Father nodded. "He's in jail."

"In jail!" Umeko cried. "But what's he done?"

Father rubbed his forehead in a gesture of weariness and concern. "He has been smuggling rice into the city for a group of black marketeers," he explained. "The police caught him last night just as he was coming out of Ueno Station."

"I was so afraid he might get into trouble," Mrs. Kagawa sighed unhappily. "I tried so often to talk to him, but, somehow, I couldn't seem to get through to him."

"What's going to happen to him?" Umeko asked anxiously. "Will he have to stay in jail very long?"

"I've made arrangements to have him released in my custody," Father said quickly. "I'll go down and pay his fine and bring him home. It's important for him to know that we have faith in him. I'll go immediately."

That evening just before supper Umeko heard the front door slide open, and she hurried out to see if Toshio had returned with Father.

"Toshio San!" she called when she saw him, "I'm so glad you're back."

Toshio looked up only briefly. "Yes, the naughty child has been brought home," he said. He smiled vaguely as he spoke, but his eyes were cold and hard. It was as though he really didn't want to be back at all.

Umeko discovered she suddenly had no words at all, and she turned quickly to go to the kitchen.

It was when they were seated at the table that Toshio said,

108

"We'd all have more to eat if the police would leave the black marketeers alone. Everybody knows it's impossible to stay alive and well on the small rations we're allowed."

"But that's not right," Umeko answered angrily. "What about the people who don't have money to buy black market food? It's because the black marketeers offer such high prices to the farmers that they hold back extra rice from the government. That's exactly what makes our rations so small."

Toshio was about to say something more, but Dr. Kagawa began to talk about his consumers' cooperatives.

"You know, the cooperatives are trying to buy food directly from the farmers and sell it at prices people can afford," he explained. "We must bring democracy and the spirit of sharing and brotherly love into our economic life, too.

"In fact," he added, "if we could only bring the cooperative technique into every phase of our lives—national and international. . . . "

He broke off suddenly with a quick grin. "I don't mean to lecture all the time," he said sheepishly.

Turning toward Toshio, Dr. Kagawa said, "We need a young man like you to go to the farmers and win their cooperation in providing our cooperatives with food. We need your help badly, Toshio San. Will you come work for us?"

Toshio put down his chopsticks and sat looking at his food.

"It would be so nice to know you were working for one of our cooperatives," Mrs. Kagawa said warmly. "Do try it for a while, won't you?"

Umeko noticed that Toshio's cheeks were flushed. He sat silent for a while and then, in a low voice, he said slowly, "No . . . I couldn't do that. I just couldn't do it." And excusing himself, he left the table abruptly. Umeko's mother started after him, but Father motioned her to stay.

"Better leave him alone," he said. "He has much to think about, and he needs to have time to straighten himself out."

Mrs. Kagawa shook her head. "If only he'd let us help him! If only he'd talk everything out instead of keeping it inside."

By next morning, however, it was too late. Toshio had taken his belongings and slipped out during the night, leaving behind only a letter on the kitchen table.

"I do not deserve your many kindnesses," he had written hurriedly. "I have not only worked with the black marketeers, I have also been working with the Communists. In fact, I've helped the Communists filter into your Consumer Cooperative so they might eventually control it for their own purposes. It is they who have fostered much of the discontent among the members lately. This is the very cooperative in which you asked me to work. Now you know I do not deserve your faith and trust. Please forgive me—miserable failure that I am. Some day, when I can earn a respectable living and can face you once more, I hope I may return. In the meantime, please know I shall always be grateful for all you have done for me. Keep well, each of you. Toshio."

Umeko shivered as her mother finished reading the letter aloud. What will he do? she wondered. Where will he go?

Father sighed deeply. "He was lost and confused, and we failed to give him the help he needed."

"Whatever made him change so?" Umeko murmured. "He is so completely different from the Toshio San we knew."

"You must remember he was young and full of brave hopes and ideals when he went off to fight," her father explained. "Then he returned, only to discover that everything he had believed in and fought for had collapsed. There was nothing left for him to turn to, and he was searching for something to fill the gap."

"And so he turned to communism?" Umeko asked.

Father nodded. "It is a pity, and a judgment on us, too, that he couldn't find hope in Christianity."

Mother shook her head. "He has rejected even that, I'm afraid," she said. "But someday perhaps he'll come back to us."

Umeko thought of the day she had talked to Toshio about her geometry. If only she had spoken to Father then, perhaps he could have made Toshio understand. But she had been too busy thinking of herself and her college exams, and now it was too late. Toshio was gone. She might never see him again.

Everything bad seemed to come at once. A few weeks later, Kazu came to see Umeko with a pale and troubled look.

"Kazu Chan!" Umeko greeted her. "It's been such a long time since I've seen you." Now that they were no longer in school together, Kazu seldom came to see her, and when they were together Umeko somehow hesitated to talk about the college Kazu hadn't been able to enter.

"I know it's been a long time," Kazu said slowly. "I should have come before, but so much has been happening." She sighed deeply and hung her head.

"What's wrong, Kazu?" Umeko asked. "What's happened?"

Kazu covered her face and began to weep softly. "Father says I must get married," she said sadly.

"Married?" Umeko shouted. "To the American soldier? To Tom San?"

Kazu shook her head and wept even harder. "Father discovered I was meeting him," she sobbed, "and now he's making me marry a man I've seen only twice."

"Oh, Kazu," Umeko gasped. "That's not right. Who is he anyway?"

"A man from Kobe," Kazu explained. "He's head of one of the education departments of Kobe City. His name is Toda

San, and he's thirty-three. Father says it's a most suitable match, and I'm lucky any man will have me."

"But why?" Umeko asked. "You're only seventeen! You've lots of time yet."

"He says when people find out I've been going out with an American soldier, no one will ever marry me. He wants me to get married before anyone finds out." Then Kazu added quickly, "But, Umeko Chan, we never did anything wrong. We just had good times together, and he was the kindest person I've ever known."

"But, Kazu, your father can't force you to marry a strange man," Umeko went on indignantly. "After all, things are different now. Tell him women aren't to be pushed around like dumb animals any more."

"Oh, I've tried, Umeko," Kazu answered. "I've talked and argued, but it's like talking to a stone wall. He's even convinced mother he's right."

"And neither of them will give in?" Umeko asked.

"Their minds are made up," Kazu said sadly. "They decided the day Father followed me and saw me meeting Tom San. I've never seen him so angry. He made me promise then that I'd never see Tom San again."

"And you haven't?" Umeko asked.

Kazu shook her head. "What's the use?" she said wanly. "It's too late. The wedding date is even set. Father had sent my photo and personal history to a friend in Kobe, and before I knew it, Toda San had arranged to come down and meet me."

Umeko leaned forward with interest. "What was he like? Was he at all nice?"

Kazu shrugged. "I scarcely remember. He was with Father's friend, and the three men did most of the talking. I served them tea, and all I remember is that Toda San wore glasses."

Kazu went on to explain that she had spent only a few hours with Toda San the next day since he had to return to Kobe to be at work on Monday.

"Oh, Kazu, we've got to get you out of this," Umeko said.

"But I can't back out now," Kazu protested. "Father couldn't embarrass his friend like that."

"Well, goodness!" Umeko persisted. "He's only the go-be-tween. It's your life that'll be ruined. Have you forgotten all the times we've talked about expressing ourselves as individuals? Now's the time to stand up for your rights."

"That's what Tom San would say, too," Kazu said sadly. "I guess I just don't have the courage you have, Umeko. I just can't disobey my parents now. They say I've brought enough shame to our family already."

Umeko felt as though she were standing by watching a friend drown. When Kazu had gone home, Umeko told her mother the whole story. "Isn't there something you can do?" she asked. "Couldn't you talk to her parents?"

Mrs. Kagawa shook her head. "Kazu's parents are doing what they think is best for her, and I can't interfere. After all," she went on, "Toda San may be a very fine man. He may be a good husband for Kazu. You can't tell, Ume Chan."

And so Umeko had to swallow the burning outrage she felt for Kazu and watch as she reluctantly made preparations for her marriage in the fall. Umeko went to see the elaborate dowry that Kazu's mother had prepared for her, admiring the silk kimono, the brocade obi, the chests of kiri wood, and the thick quilts that had been put away for Kazu.

"We were fortunate not to lose anything during the war," Mrs. Takahashi said gratefully. "Now we can provide Kazu Chan with a dowry any girl would be proud of."

113

But Kazu seemed neither pleased nor impressed. She simply sat back, watching as her parents prodded her on toward her wedding.

Kazu's father had selected a special lucky day for the ceremony, and the small shrine bustled with five other weddings besides Kazu's. As Umeko and her mother arrived, they could see another bride getting dressed for the wedding that was to follow Kazu's. Everywhere there seemed to be men in faded black cutaways that smelled of moth balls and women in formal black crested kimono that had been carefully preserved during the war years.

When Kazu came in to take her place before the white-robed priest at the small shrine, Umeko almost gasped aloud. Kazu was wearing a beautiful white silk kimono and a ceremonial headdress. Across the front of the wig was pinned the traditional strip of white cloth meant to hide the "horns of jealousy." Her face was painted a chalk white with thick layers of powder, and only the center of her lips was painted a deep dark red. She no longer looked like Kazu but like an elaborately dressed doll that breathed and moved. Her smiling rosy face was transformed as though by a mask into that of a typical Japanese bride.

Umeko remembered how she and Kazu had talked of becoming women with minds of their own. And she thought about the talks they'd had in the shelters when Kazu had said she'd rather marry a man she loved than a man of position and wealth.

And now look what's happened to her, Umeko thought bitterly. And all because she met Tom San.

There was no time to talk to Kazu after the ceremony, for she was hustled back home where the Takahashis had a small reception. They had been given a special ration of rice for the wedding, and Kazu's mother had made festive red-bean rice, apologizing profusely for the lack of food to go with it. "The food is indeed unworthy of our guests," she lamented, "but with times as they are, we hope you will understand."

There was a great deal of talk and laughter as friends and relatives were introduced and long congratulatory speeches made. But at last it was time for Kazu and her husband to leave for the station where they would catch the train to the Atami hot springs.

Umeko went with some of the relatives to wave a last good-by at the station. Kazu bowed dutifully to everyone, saying her thanks and farewells, and at last she had a moment with Umeko.

"I tried to get in to help you change your dress," Umeko said, "but you were surrounded by cousins and aunts."

"I know," Kazu said mournfully. "Wasn't it awful?"

Umeko found it hard to say good-by. "Take care of yourself," she said, pressing Kazu's hand.

Kazu nodded. "I'll miss you," she said. "Write to me!"

"I will," Umeko promised. "You write, too!"

And then, Kazu's husband was calling her. "*Sah*, we must get on board," he said, and, striding ahead quickly, he left Kazu to hurry along after him.

With a great lurch the train was off. Kazu leaned from the window waving a white handkerchief. "*Sayonara*," she called again and again. "*Sayonara . . . sayonara. . . .*" Her small high voice drifted away with the sound of the train. Umeko watched until the white handkerchief disappeared behind the cloud of smoke, and then she turned to go home.

Now Kazu was gone, too. As Umeko rode home on the crowded train, she felt an immense loneliness welling up inside. All during the long years of war, she had prayed for the war to end and for peace to come. She had believed everything would be fine then, but peace had come and brought only sadness and disappointment to two of her best friends. It was a strange frightening world.

Even Tsuda College was turning out to be something of a disappointment to Umeko. The students talked of striking for their rights and of striking in support of Communist professors who were being dismissed from other colleges in Japan. They seemed to be constantly stirring up a feeling of discontent among the students.

"Why don't we fight back?" Umeko had said to some of her classmates. "Why don't the Christian students organize, too? Why should the Communists run everything?" But the Christian students chose to keep silent. "It's not for us to get involved in political matters," they said. "Our only responsibility is to be good students. Let the Communists do as they please. We'll concentrate on our studies."

Somehow Umeko found it difficult to keep her mind on her studies, and slowly her grades began to dip.

"If you're so anxious to do something," her friends said to her, "you go ahead and talk to the Communists. You convince them they're wrong." But Umeko knew she couldn't.

"How can I make them understand?" she would say. "I couldn't even convince one of my best friends."

Umeko's confusion and disappointment grew as the weeks went by, and soon she began to wonder if she could continue at Tsuda. Somehow all her dreams and hopes seemed to be vanishing. Now she could understand something of Toshio's bewilderment. Maybe I'm going to be a failure, too, she thought.

CHAPTER TEN

U MEKO WROTE LONG LETTERS TO KAZU AND WAITED
anxiously to hear from her. But the weeks passed and
the months passed, and there was no reply.

"She's probably busy getting accustomed to her new life,"
Umeko's mother suggested. "Give her time. She'll write you."

When word came at last, however, it was only a formal
New Year's greeting card from Kazu and her husband.

"It's so strange," Umeko remarked to Miss Tanaka one
day. "Kazu Chan has simply disappeared into her new life in
Kobe and not written me once. It's just not like Kazu at all.
I keep wondering if something's wrong."

"Would you like to go and see for yourself?" Miss Tanaka
asked suddenly.

Umeko's eyes widened. "Would I? I'd give anything to see
Kazu, but that's impossible."

"And why is it so impossible?" Miss Tanaka asked. "When is your spring recess?"

Umeko knew Miss Tanaka had something in mind. "March 27 till April 8," Umeko answered quickly. "Why?"

"Well, I'd like to take you to Kobe with me then," she said calmly. "I have to go on an errand for my father to see Professor Ito at Kwansei Gakuin nearby. That won't take long, and we can go to see Kazu San afterward. In fact," she added, "we might even make a real trip of it and see the cherry blossoms in Kyoto on the way back."

"Oh, Tanaka San." Umeko said happily. "You'll really let me go along? This is the best thing that's happened to me since the war ended!"

Now the days were full of promise, for even if Umeko's studies were difficult and school sometimes seemed impossible, there was the bright prospect of spring recess, waiting for her like a golden reward. Umeko decided she would simply surprise Kazu, and she tore up the letter she had written to her.

At last it was the day to leave, and Umeko's mother went to the station with her. Umeko carried a suitcase in one hand and her lunch wrapped in a silk *furoshiki* in the other, while her mother helped with still another bundle.

"You have your toothbrush and your warm pajamas in case it gets cold?" her mother asked. "And your gift for Kazu Chan?"

Umeko nodded absently. "I have them . . . I have them," she murmured.

They hurried to Platform Three where the Osaka Express was to pull out at nine o'clock. There was still half an hour, but already the platform was crowded with people who formed lines to get on the train early and be sure of a good seat. Umeko stood on her toes to look for Miss Tanaka.

"I'll find you on the platform," she had said casually. "You just get in the shortest line, and I'll find you."

But as the crowds thickened, Umeko felt almost ill with worry. "Suppose we miss each other?" she said anxiously to her mother. "Suppose. . . . "

Someone touched her arm. "Just as I thought. You didn't even look at your ticket!" It was Miss Tanaka pulling her out of the third class line. "I knew third class would be impossibly crowded, so I got tickets for second class. I've been waiting for you at the other end of the platform," she said.

"Second class!" Umeko exclaimed. "I've never ridden on second before." She couldn't say much more, however, for Miss Tanaka was pushing her along the platform. "Hurry! We don't have too much time," she panted.

Umeko's mother hurried after them and just had time to hand Umeko the bundle she was carrying as her daughter leaped into the car. Umeko opened the window, leaned out and called, "Good-by, Mother. *Sayonara!*"

Mrs. Kagawa bowed and called out her thanks. "It is so good of you to take Umeko with you," she said to Miss Tanaka. Then the people on the platform edged up to the train windows. They bowed and waved and called as though the train were leaving for some far-distant land. Weaving among them was the little man who sold clay pots of tea. "*Ocha . . . ocha . . . ocha . . .* " he called, trying to make one more sale before the train pulled out. As the train eased out of the station at the very stroke of nine, he stopped and stood at attention like a soldier watching his general go by. The smiling faces blurred; Umeko and Miss Tanaka were on their way.

The train sped along past Yokohama, and, before long, they could see the tip of Mount Fuji looming above a mass of gray clouds.

"Ah, there it is," Miss Tanaka said. "We're lucky! Sometimes it's too cloudy to see Fuji San this time of year."

Umeko pressed her nose against the window and looked up at the hazy blue tip of Fuji towering above the square patches of wheat fields.

"It's a good omen, isn't it?" she said, and turning toward Miss Tanaka she added, "I have a feeling something good is going to come of this trip!"

Miss Tanaka smiled. "You know something, Umeko San?" she said. "I do, too."

The train wound on, past curving white beaches where the waters of the Pacific curled against the shore, past old pine trees bent by the winds, past rows and rows of neat, rounded tea plants and green, growing fields of wheat. When at last they saw the five-story towers of the Kyoto temples, they knew that before long they would be in Osaka.

Miss Tanaka had made arrangements for them to stay in a small Japanese inn in Osaka. "The inns in Kyoto are even nicer," she said, "but I think you'll like this one, Umeko San."

Umeko followed Miss Tanaka up a graveled walk to a neat little house that looked as though it might once have been someone's home, saved from the bombs and now converted into an inn. A maid bowed to greet them at the entrance and then pattered ahead of them down the polished corridor to their room. She slid open the doors at the far end, opening the room to an exquisite garden. Umeko could see that it had been made with loving and exacting care—each stone in place, azaleas in bloom, thick green moss, and water that trickled from a bamboo spout dropping softly into a curved pond. The maid hurried out and returned with a pot of hot tea and steaming towels in little oval baskets, so they might wipe their hands before they drank their tea.

"*Dozo*, please rest yourselves," she said with a bow. "And the bath is ready whenever you would like to have it."

Umeko felt as though she'd been away on a long trip during the war years and had only now come back to Japan. "I didn't think anyone lived like this any more," she said. "It seems almost old fashioned."

"But it's nice, don't you think?" Miss Tanaka asked. "You know, even if Japan did much that was wrong during the war, she still does have a way of life that is beautiful and serene and good."

Umeko nodded. "It is peaceful," she agreed.

They took hot baths in the big square wooden tub and changed to cotton kimono the maid laid out for them. Then, as they watched the moon appear over their little garden, the maid returned with their supper on two black trays.

"With rationing, it is difficult to prepare anything very tasty," she apologized. But to Umeko the supper seemed a sumptuous banquet. She sighed happily. "I'd almost forgotten how nice a Japanese inn could be," she confessed.

"I'm sure you had," Miss Tanaka agreed. "I'm afraid most young people have forgotten how nice many Japanese things can be," she added. "They've been too busy becoming Westernized."

Umeko was puzzled. "What do you mean?"

"Oh, they've swarmed to American movies, they've learned to dance and hold hands in public, and they've become rude and irresponsible and disobedient to their elders, thinking freedom and democracy mean all this."

Umeko knew she and Kazu had been guilty of many of the same thoughts. "Well," she said defiantly, "is that so wrong? I thought you approved of our new freedom."

"Oh, I do," Miss Tanaka added. "But we must use it wisely and absorb it gradually." Miss Tanaka took a deep breath and leaned on the little armrest beside her cushion. "You see, Umeko San," she began, "you young people want to make everything black and white, but everything Japanese isn't necessarily bad and everything Western isn't always good. You've got to be discriminating and choose the good from both."

Umeko silently pondered what Miss Tanaka was saying.

"I know this may sound strange coming from me, especially when you've heard me talk so much about freedom for Japan's women," she went on, "but think it over and see if you don't agree."

Long after they had turned out the lights and lay on the thick quilts, listening to the drip-drip of water in the pond outside the night shutters, Umeko thought of the things Miss Tanaka had said to her. "Perhaps that's one of my troubles," she concluded. "I've always wanted things to be black or white." Father had once said that to her, too. Perhaps she and Kazu had tried too hard to become independent and free.

It seemed she had just dropped off when the morning sun was streaming into the room and Miss Tanaka was whistling Beethoven in her ear. "Get up, lazy one!" she said. "We've got to be at Professor Ito's by ten o'clock."

They barely had time to rush to the station to catch the train for Nishinomiya, and when they arrived at Professor Ito's office, he was already there waiting for them.

"Ah, come in. *Dozo*, come in," he called to them. He shook Miss Tanaka's hand warmly and then turned to Umeko. "And you are Kagawa San. Yes, Tanaka San told me you would be coming with her."

He looked at Umeko with a kind smile and beckoned them both to sit down. Umeko liked him immediately. He had a friendly, rumpled look, somewhat like her own father. He wore a heavy black suit that looked two sizes too large for him, and Umeko wondered if perhaps it had come in a relief bundle from America. It almost looked as though he hadn't even bothered to press it after taking it from the box.

As Miss Tanaka talked to the professor, Umeko looked about the room. There were books everywhere, filling the shelves that covered every wall and seeming to grow right up from the floor in large, unwieldly stacks. From time to time, as he talked with Miss Tanaka, the professor would reach for a volume, always knowing just where to find the right one. He scribbled constantly, making notes on little slips of paper, nodding and writing comments on the papers Miss Tanaka placed before him.

At last he smiled happily. "There," he said, like a child who had completed his homework, "we've finished. And now, come," he said to Umeko, "pull up your chair and tell me what you are doing. You go to Tsuda, don't you?"

"Yes, I do," Umeko answered. "I've just completed my first year."

"And you are enjoying it there?" he asked, tilting his head to one side.

"Yes . . . yes, I am," Umeko began, but as she looked at Professor Ito's earnest face, she knew she wanted to be truthful with him. "Well, no, not really," she admitted. "In fact, I've been rather unhappy there."

"So?" answered the professor. "Tell me about it. What is troubling you?"

Miss Tanaka gave her an encouraging smile. Umeko took a deep breath and suddenly she found herself unburdening all her troubles to the old gentleman. "I just feel so mixed up about everything," she said. "I'm even making a mess of my studies."

"Ah, but that is natural," Professor Ito interrupted. "It is a time of confusion and upheaval for us all."

"But that isn't all," Umeko went on, and she told him how frustrated she felt watching the Communist students dominate activities at school, not being able to stop them or even talk to them. "I just don't know how to defend my own beliefs," she said. "I want to tell those other students they're wrong, but I don't seem to have the right words!"

Professor Ito nodded with understanding. "It's not easy, Kagawa San," he said gently. "The Communists are a big problem for all of us Christians in Japan, adult and student alike. It is a problem even in the high schools now. But one thing I can tell you for certain is that you must study hard. You must acquaint yourself with the beliefs of the Communists so you will understand what it is you want to fight. And you must study the Bible and the teachings of Jesus and fully realize the importance of the church in our lives."

"Oh, but I have read the Bible," Umeko interrupted, "and I have gone to Sunday school for years and years!"

Professor Ito smiled. "You have only scratched the surface," he said patiently. "Only the surface. You must study and work even harder. You young people are the hope of Japan. Through you we must bring Christian love and hope to our nation."

"But we're so mixed up now," Umeko went on. "We've had freedom and democracy thrown at us so suddenly, and so far it seems to have brought more unhappiness than anything else—at least to my friends."

Professor Ito stood up now and pointed an accusing finger at Umeko. "Ah," he said, "because you have failed to accept the responsibility that must come with freedom. For every right, there is also a duty. Don't you see, my dear," he went on, "liberty does not mean freedom to go in all directions at once. It means freedom to choose one right way. It means working for truth and justice and goodness."

He had begun to pace back and forth now. It was as though he had forgotten both Umeko and Miss Tanaka. He talked as if he were facing a room full of young students.

"You must seek to uphold these basic values cherished by free countries the world over," he said, "and you must work hard to help apply them to our own culture. It won't be easy, for our history is different, and we must preserve our own fine culture, too."

Suddenly Professor Ito stopped and smiled sheepishly. "What am I doing?" he said, sitting down, "I'm lecturing to you when I should be listening to you."

"Oh, but you've been very helpful to Umeko San, I'm sure," Miss Tanaka said.

The professor shook his head. "I get so impatient," he said. "There is so much to be done in Japan. There is such an urgent need for good new leadership."

As Umeko listened she knew that Professor Ito was the person who could help straighten her out. She suddenly found herself asking, "Would it be possible for me to come here to study with you? Now that your school is coeducational, I mean. . . ."

Professor Ito looked pleased. A slow smile spread over his face, and he bowed slightly toward Umeko.

"I should indeed be delighted to have you," he said, "but, first, you must consult your parents and see if they are willing. If, after that, you'd still like to come, write me a letter, and we'll make the necessary arrangements for your transfer."

Umeko felt that at last she was climbing out from the marsh in which she had wallowed all year. Coming to Kwansei Gakuin would truly be a new beginning for her. She would have a chance to live away from home and be on her own. Umeko knew it was something she simply had to do.

"Tanaka San," she said breathlessly as they left Professor Ito, "what do you think? Do you think it's a good idea, my coming here?"

"I couldn't think of a better idea if I'd thought of it myself," Miss Tanaka replied.

Umeko saw the satisfied smile that crept over Miss Tanaka's face, and suddenly a thought occurred to her. "Maybe you did think of it yourself," she exclaimed. "Did you?"

Miss Tanaka continued to smile. "Well, I admit I did want you to meet Professor Ito. I had a feeling something good would come of it, but, truthfully, Umeko San, I had no idea it would be this good!"

Umeko took Miss Tanaka's arm. "You're a wonderful friend," she said happily.

Miss Tanaka looked down at her watch. "We just have time for a bowl of noodles, and then we'll find Kazu San," she said.

Finding Kazu's house, however, was not so simple as they'd expected. "Kobe has changed so after the bombings, I hardly know it any more," Miss Tanaka said as they wandered from one narrow street to another. "I think I'm completely lost."

Umeko stopped at a little shop where a man was boiling white squares of bean curd in an enormous wooden barrel. "Excuse me," she said, "I wonder if you might help us find this address." She held out Kazu's address written on a piece of paper and waited as the man squinted at it.

"Sah . . . , " he murmured, scratching his head and sucking the breath between his teeth. "I think this must be beyond the bath house. You can see the chimney down the road. I think this must be just on the edge of the Shinkawa District."

"The Shinkawa District," Umeko repeated. "Are we near there? Are we near the settlement house?"

The man nodded. "Ah, the settlement house, yes. It is just down the street. Turn right at the bath house and left at the red mailbox."

"Perhaps someone at the settlement house could help us find Kazu San," Miss Tanaka suggested.

Soon they were walking past shabby wooden houses with sagging roofs and battered boards and bamboo poles full of washing strung across each window. There was a vague odor of refuse about the street and dirty children with runny noses seemed to dart about everywhere, playing in puddles that the rain had left on the unpaved street. Umeko wrinkled her nose in distaste. "There it is," she said, pointing to the settlement house.

They went inside the two-story wooden building, shuffling down the dark hallway in the big straw slippers provided at the entrance. Suddenly a screaming child bolted from a doorway and sprawled on the floor as he ran into Umeko. A woman came quickly after him, taking him in her arms to comfort him.

"Taka Chan is new to our kindergarten and still tries to run home," she explained. Then, looking at the child, she went on, "But we know Mother isn't home because she's out working, don't we?"

The child nodded and the woman, still speaking softly to him, led him back to the kindergarten. She returned quickly to Umeko and Miss Tanaka. "Now," she said cheerfully, "may I help you?"

When Umeko told her who they were, her face crumpled into a happy smile, and she insisted on showing them the entire building. "We need so much more room, but more than that," she explained, looking hopefully at Umeko, "we need trained social workers. We're looking forward to the time when you'll be helping us."

"Oh, I'm still in school," Umeko said quickly, "and, besides, I may not go into . . . that is . . . I'm not sure just what I'll do when I graduate." Why did everyone take it for granted that she would follow in her father's footsteps?

The woman looked embarrassed. "Oh, of course," she said, "it's just that I see the need and become so eager."

Umeko saw the disappointment that flooded her face and was sorry she'd spoken as she did, but it was too late.

Miss Tanaka changed the subject and inquired about finding Kazu's house.

"Toda, Kazu San?" the woman asked. "Why, yes, I know her. She comes to our sewing class. She lives just a short way down the street."

Umeko was surprised. Somehow she hadn't expected Kazu to live in a neighborhood like this one. They thanked the woman and followed her directions down the narrow street. They came to a long building that housed several families, and at the far end there was a name plate marked "Toda."

"This must be it," Umeko said, and for a moment she almost wished she hadn't come. Perhaps Kazu had a reason for keeping silent so long. Perhaps she didn't want anyone to find her in such a place.

"I wish I'd written her first," she said, pausing beside the door. But Miss Tanaka urged her on. "Don't back down now," she said. "Open the door."

Umeko slid open the door and called, "Excuse me. Is anyone home? . . . Kazu Chan?" It was dark inside for the sun didn't penetrate far in these long buildings. Umeko blinked as she tried to see in the darkness. "Kazu Chan?" she called again.

There was the sound of bare feet hurrying on the *tatami*, and then there was Kazu herself, drying her hands on the big white apron she wore. "Umeko Chan!" she cried disbelieving. "What are you doing here?"

"Why, I . . . I came to Osaka on a trip with Tanaka San," she said, flustered. She hardly knew what to say. Kazu seemed embarrassed and almost frightened, like an animal discovered in its hiding place. For a moment Umeko thought Kazu might cry, but soon she spoke slowly, "Our house is so small and dirty. I'm afraid you will be shocked."

"But, Kazu San, you will let us come in for just a minute, won't you?" Miss Tanaka interrupted. "My feet hurt so from walking in these high heels. I simply must sit down."

Kazu smiled for the first time. "Of course," she said, "I've been very rude. Do come in. I can at least make you a cup of tea."

When they were seated on the small silk cushions that Kazu produced from the closet, she at last seemed pleased to see them.

"It's so good to see you," Umeko began, "but why haven't you written? It's been months since you left Tokyo."

"I know," Kazu answered dejectedly, "but just look at me—living in these two small rooms with my husband and his mother and sister, cooking over my little charcoal burner, washing at the outdoor pump, and learning to sew at night. When I do have time to write, I'm too tired."

"But, Kazu Chan, I thought . . . I thought your husband . . . ," Umeko began.

"I know," Kazu interrupted. "I thought he had a big house, too. I thought he was a department head at the City Hall, but he's only a clerk. All those things he told us were miserable lies!"

"But didn't your father's friend check on all this?" Miss Tanaka asked. "Wasn't he your go-between?"

"He was fooled, too," Kazu said darkly. "If Father hadn't been in such a hurry, we could have been more careful."

Umeko glanced around the dismal, shabby room. The paper on the sliding doors was torn and needed changing, the walls were streaked, and the ceiling was spotted with rain.

"Is it all right for you to talk like this?" Umeko asked cautiously. "Won't someone hear you?"

"It's all right," Kazu said quickly. "Mother is at the doctor's, and my sister-in-law is working. I'm home alone."

"Oh, Kazu Chan," Umeko blurted out, "I had no idea you were living like this. Is your husband good to you?"

Kazu shrugged. "He means well. He is quiet and obeys his mother like a child. She is the one who planned all this. Now she has a housekeeper and someone to earn extra money with sewing." Kazu paused and looked at Umeko. "This is my fine free postwar world!" she said bitterly.

"But there must be something we can do for you," Miss Tanaka said. "You could always return home."

Kazu shook her head. "My parents don't know," she said, "and they would never allow me to return to my home even if they knew how unhappy I am. I know I can never hope for anything better."

"Kazu San, you must never lose hope," Miss Tanaka said.

Kazu shook her head. "I am exactly like my country—poor, hungry, and beaten."

As Umeko listened, she remembered what Professor Ito had said that morning about Christian hope. If only she could tell Kazu about it. Umeko was filled with the same helplessness she felt when Toshio had talked to her with such bitterness. This time she simply couldn't let Kazu down.

"Listen, Kazu Chan," she said. "I'm going to see more of you next year. You are my best friend, and I'm not going to desert you. I'll be back to help you somehow. I promise."

Kazu simply smiled, and her voice became gentle as she said, "It was good to see you, Umeko Chan."

The hurried sound of geta filled the street outside as Umeko and Miss Tanaka rose to leave. The shadows were lengthening, and housewives were hurrying to buy a piece of fish or a long white radish to cook for dinner.

Kazu slipped on her geta and came outside with them. She stood like a small child, watching and waving until Umeko and Miss Tanaka turned at the bend of the road.

As Umeko looked back, she felt tears sting at her eyes. She walked along silently, looking up at the thin white curve of the moon in the lavender-gray sky. "I am going to help them," she said with determination, as if to convince Miss Tanaka that she had meant what she said to Kazu.

"Help whom?" Miss Tanaka asked.

"Kazu . . . the settlement worker . . . the girls who live at the settlement . . . , " Umeko said slowly. "All of them."

"Ah, the full circle at last," Miss Tanaka said almost to herself.

Umeko turned to her, puzzled. "What did you say?"

"Remember how you used to talk to me about wanting to become free and independent? How you felt that too much was being asked of you as the daughter of Toyohiko Kagawa?" Miss Tanaka asked.

Umeko nodded. "I remember, and I'm still a rebel."

"I know," Miss Tanaka said nodding, "you still think you're running away from your father, but now, at last, you're both going in the same direction. It's just that you had to have your own separate path. Don't you see, Umeko, you're finding a way to express yourself and still be your father's daughter?"

Suddenly the words her father had quoted to her time and time again came to Umeko's mind: " . . . whosoever will be great among you . . . shall be servant of all." Even when Father had appeared before the Emperor and Empress, he had told them, "Only through service to others can a man or nation find true peace."

It had taken her a long time to realize what her father had been trying to tell her all these years, but, now at last, the meaning of his words began to come clear.

During the next two days, as she and Miss Tanaka visited the quiet temples and gardens of Kyoto, Umeko thought again and again about her new plans. It would be so wonderful to study with Professor Ito, to seek the solutions to her problems, and to be able, somehow, to help Kazu. And, someday, perhaps she might even see Toshio again. This time she was sure she would be able to help him understand, and maybe. when she finished at Kwansei Gakuin, the Umeko who had fought so long to be free would find her dreams realized in work outside the shell of herself. Then, as Miss Tanaka said, perhaps the circle would be complete.

"But maybe this is just another of my big dreams," Umeko said a bit doubtfully to Miss Tanaka. "Suppose the selfish me pops up again and all this doesn't amount to anything at all?"

Miss Tanaka put a hand on her arm and said softly, "Don't worry, Umeko San. Perhaps it is only a dream, but you hold on to it because it's a good dream—a very good dream. And who knows? It's just possible that some day it may come true."

Umeko nodded thoughtfully. Perhaps it might at that.

NOTES

DR. TOYOHIKO KAGAWA, ONE OF JAPAN'S GREAT CHRISTIAN EVANGE-
lists, has been for many years the champion of the unloved and
oppressed people of Japan. His devotion to the service of others
is almost universally known. Dr. Kagawa has always chosen to
"work in the most difficult fields and not be afraid." When he
was a young man, he lived in the squalor of the Kobe slums and
brought the deplorable conditions there to the attention of the
Japanese government. Seeing the pathetic plight of Japan's laborers
and peasants, he tried to bring dignity and hope into their lives
through labor unions and farm reforms.

Imprisoned many times, not only for his attempted reforms but
also for his pacifism, Dr. Kagawa has stoutly upheld his belief that
love can overcome the need for all violence. He has helped establish countless churches, cooperatives, settlements, gospel schools,
and orphanages. He has written many books—prose and poetry.
And, of course, he has never ceased in his efforts to win the Japanese people to Jesus Christ.

After finishing Kwansei Gakuin University, Umeko was awarded
a Fulbright Travel Grant. She came to the United States in 1952
to study at the General Assembly's Training School for Lay Workers in Richmond, Virginia, and later at Yale Divinity School in
New Haven, Connecticut. On her way back to Japan, she spent
part of one summer in a work camp at Vellitry, Italy. Now in
Japan she is teaching a class of junior high girls in the Matsuzawa
Church in Tokyo and seeking opportunities to work more actively
with Japan's growing community of Christian students.

GLOSSARY

GUIDE TO PRONUNCIATION

Consonants: sounded, generally, as in English, except g is always hard as in gift

Vowels:
a as in calm	ai or ay as in aisle
e as in get	au or ou as in plow
i as in if	ei as in eight
o as in no	oi as in oil
u as in bull	the final e is always sounded

GLOSSARY

arigato	thank you
banzai	similar to "three cheers"
Chan	term of endearment frequently added to a child's name when speaking to him informally, thus Umeko's mother called her "Ume Chan"
domo arigato gozai mashita	thank you very much
dozo	please
furoshiki	two-foot or three-foot square of cloth in which small objects are wrapped and carried
gemma	pledge to keep one's promise
geta	wooden clogs
gomen kudasai	excuse me
hai	yes
haiku	short seventeen syllable Japanese poem
happi	short loose coat made of cotton and usually worn by laborers
kimono	Japanese dress
mah, mah	exclamation, similar to "my, my!" or "my goodness!"

mompei	loose work trousers worn in the fields by rural women and used by most Japanese women during the war years
ocha	tea
ochugen	midsummer gift
ohayo	good morning
omedeto gozai masu	literally, "congratulations," but it can also be used to mean "Happy New Year"
sah	exclamation similar to "come!" or "come now!" but according to the inflection, it can also mean "let's see," as in Chapter Ten
San	can be used to mean "Mr.," "Mrs.," or "Miss" in addressing anyone. The Japanese rarely address anyone without adding "San" to his name. In this book "San" has been omitted occasionally in informal conversation
sayonara	good-by
sensei	teacher, a term of respect used in addressing or referring to someone like Dr. Kagawa
shoji	sliding doors that divide Japanese rooms, made of paper mounted on wooden frames
sutra	Buddhist teachings
tadaima	greeting used on returning home, meaning "I'm home."
tatami	woven rush mats that serve as floor covering in most Japanese homes

TEXT SET IN 11 POINT ELECTRA LEADED 3 POINTS
COMPOSITION AND PRINTING BY SOWERS PRINTING COMPANY
BINDING BY BOOK CRAFTSMEN ASSOCIATES
COVERS AND JACKETS BY AFFILIATED LITHOGRAPHERS, INC.

Typographic design by Dorothy Papy
Binding design by Louise E. Jefferson